Plane Geometry

and Other Affairs of the Heart

Illinois State University / Fiction Collective Series

CURTIS WHITE, *Series Editor*

Plane Geometry

and Other Affairs of the Heart

R. M. BERRY

ILLINOIS STATE UNIVERSITY

Normal

FICTION COLLECTIVE

New York

PS
3552
.E748
P56
1985

Library of Congress Cataloging in Publication Data

Berry, R. M.
Plane geometry and other affairs of the heart.

I. Illinois State University/Fiction Collective (U.S.) II. Title.
PS3552.E748P56 1985   813'.54   84-8172
ISBN 0-914590-88-X
ISBN 0-914590-89-8 (pbk.)

Grateful acknowledgement is made to the following magazines where these stories first appeared: *Carolina Quarterly* for "A Circle is the Shape of Perfection" and *West Branch* for "November 14, 1864."

This publication is the 1984 winner of the Illinois State University/Fiction Collective Award, jointly sponsored by the Illinois State University Fine Arts Festival and the Fiction Collective.

Published by Illinois State University/Fiction Collective with support from Illinois State University, the National Endowment for the Arts, and the New York State Council on the Arts, and with the cooperation of Brooklyn College and Teachers & Writers Collaborative.

In addition, this publication is made possible, in part, with public funds from the Greater New York Arts Development Fund, a project of the New York City Department of Cultural Affairs, as administered in Kings County by the Brooklyn Arts and Culture Association, Inc. (BACA).

My thanks to artist Nana Burford for her help with the geometer's apples on page 44 and to Daniel Campion who proofread the text with a zeal and precision that staggers belief.

The "encyclopedia" entries in "Apples" are composites of factual material plundered, jumbled and plagiarized from: *Funk & Wagnalls Standard Dictionary of Folklore, Mythology and Legend: Taylor's Encyclopedia of Gardening*; the *Dictionary of Mythology, Folklore, and Symbols* by Gertrude Jobes; the *Encyclopedia Britannica Micropedia*; the *New York Botanical Garden Illustrated Encyclopedia of Horticulture* by Thomas Everett; *Hortus Third: A Concise Dictionary of Plants of Horticulture* by L. H. Bailey (vol. I); and Voltaire's *Letters on the English Nation*.

Text design: McPherson & Company
Cover and jacket design: Andrius Balukas
Author photograph: Randall Tosh

Cover detail from "The Geographer" by Jan Vermeer van Delft, reproduced with the permission of Städelsches Kunstinstitut Frankfurt.

Manufactured in the United States of America.

Typeset by Open Studio in Rhinebeck, N.Y., a non-profit facility for writers, artists and independent literary publishers, supported in part by grants from the New York State Council on the Arts and the National Endowment for the Arts.

For SRH,
who was there.

C O N T E N T S

Their ideas are perpetually conversant in lines and figures. If they would, for example, praise the beauty of a woman or any other animal, they describe it by rhombs, circles, parallelograms, ellipses, and other geometrical terms, or else by words of art drawn from music, needless here to repeat.

Gulliver's Travels

SONG OF THE GEOMETRY INSTRUCTOR

Everyone remembers the winter you left me, Hazel. It was the winter of the great Pensacola blizzard, the winter of the twelve-foot drifts and killing winds, of the northern Florida ice shelf and the mass migrations to Biloxi, San Antonio, and the Keys. It was the winter when everyone stopped sleeping and sat watching the snow pile up in the azaleas, when I lived on canned peaches and zwieback and the phones went out and the TV went out and our mail wouldn't come.

Not our mail. My mail. An old habit. Even now I must remember to correct old habits.

Has all that been a year ago, Hazel? Has it been five? Perhaps it was last Thursday that I stood on the stoop, my hands stuffed deep into my pockets, and gazed out over the walk as, turning, you tossed your blood-brown hair for what I thought would surely be the last time but was really only the essential time, and left it there, tossing in the empty air while you drove away.

It stayed there for a long time, until the drifts got so high that I couldn't see it anymore. And even then, buried inside the house with the snow packing silently about me, I knew that it was there and that if I were to dig my way out of the living room and push a tunnel through the drifts and somehow shovel the walk clear again that I would still find it, your blood-brown hair, whipping, slapping about your neck in the empty air.

No, Hazel, no one will ever forget that winter. My students that winter were the best students I'd ever had. We covered rhombi, trapezoids, and parallelograms in September, cones, octahedrons, and hexahedrons by October's end, had determined genetrix and directrix, parameters and curves, and were already beginning ellipses, hyperboloids, and paraboloids when in mid-November the snows began.

I still remember the last class, the students' upturned faces floating just below my hands like white flakes. I knew that by morning the snows would be too deep for me to come back, but at the time I could think of nothing but the shapes I hadn't made possible for my students, all the theorems, postulates, and proofs they still didn't own. The flake-like faces waited as I tried to conjure from thought the last series of numbers and signs, but the freeze was already setting in. I watched the drifts edging up the windows. In a matter of hours everything would be buried. Surely my students understood that there was nothing more I could do.

Pensacola was the coldest place on record anywhere in North America that winter, colder than Fairbanks, Halifax, or Montreal. Plate glass windows cracked from the cold; thermometers frosted over; people walked three blocks then simply froze up. You'd come on them standing there and could tell if it had happened quickly or slowly by the expressions on their faces. Their eyes would be milky gray with fine cracks wrinkling out from the pupils. The fingers would break off. Noses would be caked on the windward side with ice.

By the time I realized that you would not be right back, that this time you were going to teach me a lesson, the snow had reached the window sills. Some houses were already lost by then in the drifts. Nobody could tell a street from a train station or a park. Everywhere people were giving up. They stopped shoveling, left their cars to freeze, quit going to work. Some joined the migration, others shrugged, went inside... died, I guess.

But not me. I kept working. Every morning I spread my compasses, protractor, triangles, curves, pencils, graphs, and tablets out on the kitchen table, piled my books up around me, plugged in my calculator and began to figure. I would warm up with a few cylinders, cones, and parallelepipeds and then go on to polyhedrons and ellipses. I used to tell myself that I could calculate the surface area of a hyperbolic paraboloid faster than any computer on the Gulf coast.

I was still working on the projection problem then, remember? The one with the helix. I felt certain that from this equation my students and I could extrapolate a whole new family of formulae and constructions. But progress was slow. I could get as far as the bending helix, the helix which twisted up to form another helix, but after that step I would become confused. To even conceive a figure, Hazel, not only of infinite extension itself but one which created by its extension a second figure also of infinite extension which in turn created another such figure infinitely extended, and to continue in this fashion so that ultimately not only is extension infinite but generation as well... to conceive such a thing is to drive thought to its knees. I could almost glimpse the near edge of the problem some mornings, like a huge shining scaffold against the blackness of space, fluorescent lines falling away to reveal curves, curves forming crystalline figures which then flared like great white novas to reveal thin lines again, a phantasmagoria of shapes. But when I would try to put it on paper, it would fade. Not shatter or crash or burst. Just fade.

dnv $(f_1, f_2, f_3, \ldots) \cdot W^* = C$

dnv $(f_1) = 4X_1$

dnv $(f_1, f_2) = 17X_2{}^2 + (?)X_2X_1 - 11X$ (or, $\dfrac{(X_2 \cdot X_1)^2}{6X}$)

dnv $(f_1, f_2, f_3) = (?)$

(converge to polynomial in $X_1, X_2, \ldots$?) $\dfrac{17 + (?)}{X_3} + X_2{}^2 \pm X_1 - 11$ (or ?)

$\ldots X_n$?

dnv $(f_1, f_2, f_3, \ldots f_n) =$ does not compute.

That much, then nothing.

But I never got frustrated. I simply clicked off the light and turned on the stereo (it was still working then) and sat listening to Dohnanyi or Milhaud or Berg or Villa-Lobos until the shimmer came back and everything—chairs, lamps, my shoes, the coffee table—became part of one figure, a crystalline net of angles and curves, each twisting into the other, and slowly my eyes closed and my body floated and I went to sleep.

Oh, Hazel, I've invented so many new shapes. You'd love the new shapes. Shapes, Hazel, you wouldn't believe.

By the end of December I had to go around the house wrapped in a down comforter. I tied towels around my feet and kept the purple cap you knitted for me pulled over my ears. I managed to keep pretty warm that way most of the time, except when I went into the bedroom. There must have been a leak in the bedroom, Hazel, or a crack in the wall. When the bureau froze up I had to get my undershorts out with a hatchet, and if I sat on the bed, I'd stick. I finally had to seal the room off. I closed up the vents, pulled some drawers into the living room, locked the door and nailed over the cracks. I spread out some blankets on the den floor for a bed—I wasn't as cold there, though the floor was pretty hard—and I relieved myself out a window into a hole I had made in the snow.

The mail had already stopped coming by then, and the phone went dead pretty early, too. (That's why I never got your calls.) But the radio kept working well into January. I left it on constantly, partly because of the weather forecasts but mostly because, now that the drifts were above the windows, the time announcements were my only way of telling day from night. Whenever the weatherman wished me good morning, I would stop whatever I was doing, stretch, go to the front door, open it, take a deep breath of the packed snow and come back to the kitchen to hear the forecast.

Up until the final broadcast the stations kept on announcing that the storm would end soon, though who could have believed them? The announcer, that last day, was predicting cloudless skies, tapering snow fall, a warming trend—the same message I had been hearing since November—when he was interrupted by static. You could tell that he heard it, too, because he paused mid-sentence, then started again very slowly. He began to explain how all the indicators pointed to an early spring and was trying to describe how these indicators were interpreted, when the static hit again, only this time much louder. "Seems like something in the stratosphere wants to argue with—" and those were the last words he said. I turned down the volume and left the radio hissing into the silent room.

Sometimes I wondered, Hazel, what would have happened if your car hadn't started. What if your hair had hung there in the air, tossing, just long enough for you to give up on the ignition, climb out of the car, and coming back across the walk, to allow it to settle again about your neck? We would have had supper then, wouldn't we? I would have opened the La Tour-Martillac, and you would have covered our plates with small, raw, faintly tart sea animals, and we would have eaten without forks, and licked each other's fingers clean, and wiped our mouths on our shirts, and afterwards I would have scraped my nail across the nipple of your rough, taut tit.

But your car was very reliable, Hazel. I never knew it not to start.

My students were becoming very important for me now, and often I imagined talking with them as I worked. They would sit around me in the kitchen and ask me to explain each process of my calculations and what it meant. As you might guess, I enjoyed this a great deal. They were learning to see space for the first time, to feel themselves moving through it, and sense its power over them. This was the finest part of all. I would show them my calculations and explain these processes, these palpable things in which we moved and breathed. Just think, I explained to them, everything we know we know within this. For knowing belongs to it. And then I would point to the half-finished equation and say, "These are its laws. These are thought's shadows on the wall of space." And their eyes would swell, and their small torsos would lean forward, and we would all stare wordlessly at the wonders of geometry.

But oddly enough, about this time I began to have difficulty with my calculations. Though I could glimpse the scaffolding of the problem now more clearly than ever before, I had trouble concentrating on it. One entire side of the figure hovered before me as I worked, and I was able to hold parts of it motionless for a few seconds, at times could even stare at it. And the equation was becoming clearer. But the lines and curves no longer shone or vanished or spun past. Their translucence had been replaced by a dusty opacity. Everything seemed simpler, but brittle.

I soon found that I was having to force myself to work, that I had to sneak up on my calculations or slip into them in some indirect way. I would come to the kitchen table each morning, would sharpen all my pencils, switch on my calculator, sweep the erasures from the table, rearrange my books, graph a few binomials, shuffle through the previous day's papers and would waste long minutes meticulously sketching sections of constructions or composite figures. Eventually this self-indulgence would make me feel foolish, and I would reach across the table for the yellow tablets of equations like a poor swimmer grasping for a boat. But self-discipline alone soon proved inadequate. I would become frustrated after only a few hours. When I sat before the stereo, I hardly knew the *Babi Yar* of Shostakovich from Strauss' *Zarathustra*. If I dozed, I woke with a start.

That was when I realized I would have to move into the cellar. The kitchen had gotten so cold that I found myself shivering as I calculated. I would hug the down comforter to my chest with one hand as I worked, and after I had put away my sketches each day, I would feel my fingers growing numb. The furnace was simply not powerful enough to warm the living room, kitchen, and den, and none of these rooms could be closed off effectively. I began to make preparations, cleared a living space, carried a mattress down to be used for a bed, put a bulb in the socket over my old workbench, hooked up the stereo in a corner beside the stairs. I had to spend considerable time modifying the furnace's duct system but finally managed to redirect all the warm air through an opening just above the bench. In the far corner of the basement at the top of the wall was a small window, buried now under a dozen feet of drifted snow. There was no door. The earth beyond the walls provided excellent insulation.

Often these days I wondered where you were, Hazel, and laughed to think how surprised you'd be if you came back and saw me there, huddled up in the cellar with the heat duct blowing against my cheek. But, of course, you couldn't have come back then. The snow was already too deep. Still, I was careful to do as little permanent damage to the house and furniture as possible. I took notes on where I placed the heat ducts and how to repair them. When I closed off the doors, I didn't drive any nails in up to the head. I swept the cellar floor before putting the mattress down. But I admit that I did begin to get depressed. It seemed so strange living under the ground beneath the snow, and I began to be afraid that I was the only survivor, that no one else in all of northern Florida had survived the cold. I worried especially about you. I was certain you had left town, and since the snow didn't begin until you were gone, I figured you were safe. But I knew you would be concerned about me. What would you think, I wondered, when your phone calls didn't connect and your letters were returned? You would surely have seen the weather reports and might fear the worst. Sometimes I imagined you trying to fight your way to me through the blizzard, pushing your car into the wind and ice until it refused to go any further, yet still forcing yourself, leaving the car behind, struggling through the snow as the drifts crept higher and higher up your legs.

Then one day an extraordinary thing happened. I was sitting at my workbench—for even in the cellar I was still trying to work— tracing a series of interpenetrating dodecahedrons, prisms, ellipsoids, and cones, when my eyes began to ache. I sat back in my chair and rubbed them. The light was not very bright, and I assumed they were tired. The stereo was playing Bartok's second piano concerto, and in the adagio movement where the piano plays pianissimo in the treble and the strings hardly seem to move at all, I closed my eyes and let myself float out onto the sound. All at once the scaffold appeared before me. Hazel, you can imagine my surprise. It rose up immense, even boundless, yet entire—no longer truncated as before—and flashing, spinning, silver as a thistle of ice. I watched as its network of lines dissolved into explosions of light revealing crystalline figures, trapezoidahedrons, pentadecagons, shining conic tri-sections, all slipping smoothly in and out of one another and spinning off into coils within coils within coils. I leaned into my eyelids. How had I thought to tether such a figure to laws and signs? I saw my equations breaking loose as the curves twisted past, watched as divisors, exponents, coefficients, and radicands snapped off and tumbled into indigo depthless space.

And suddenly I was moving. I shoved my tablets aside, turned the stereo up loud, tore some twine from a book box, broke the straw off a partially rotted broom, scavenged a bag of flour and five drinking straws from the kitchen, gathered tissue paper, monofilament line, paper clips and hair pins and from an old valise of art supplies pulled a snotty-nosed bottle of mucilage and an unopened tube of modeler's dope.

Weissenberg—for I was listening to the Weissenberg recording—was beating on the part just before the allegro molto, the part that you once called Bella Lugosi's entrance. The bam-baumm boom, bum part. I sat back down at the bench and gazed about me at the piles of erratic shapes, minute, faintly sinister forms in the dim light. To one side of me sprawled the overlong yellow tablets of my equations, and I thought how jaundiced they looked. I felt a cool palpitation of laughter just below my diaphragm but made no sound. Bartok died of penury and bad leukocytes, I thought. I looked at my smudged calculations. Béla Lugosi. And then I did laugh. Slowly, methodically, I crushed the sheets and tablets into a shoe box, and holding the lid closed, crossed to the window, opened it quickly, and crammed the box into the loosely packed snow.

Then I began to work. I started with quadrilaterals and simple polyhedrons, making them from broom straw and flour paste, limiting myself to very small sizes, so small you could hold a trapezoid, a rhombus, and a prism in your palm at once. I measured precise lengths of straw, snapped them at the mark, formed tiny ells and vees and square yews which when dry and hard could be fitted into place until the figures tottered like slender animals with missing limbs, then gradually raised themselves on fours, and then, as with the hexahedrons which came later or the pentadecahedrons or finally the prismatic paraboloids, on sixes, eights or even odd combinations of nines, sevens and threes, raising themselves like waking men, lifting their heads, stretching, until at last they stood erect. Weissenberg gave way to Tashi, and Tashi to La Goya, to the Berlin playing Smetana, to Heifetz and Ashkenazy and the Guarneri and Entremont and Steinberg and Fodor and the old Budapest recordings and finally to Rafael Kubelik and Mahler's fifth symphony. I sat listening to the strings in the fourth movement, the adagietto, the scarcely bearable attenuation of every longing in the world, as around me the tiny shapes piled up, bright and fragile and as weightless as thought.

Oh, Hazel, if you could have seen the forms filling up the basement, standing about on fruit crates and garden hoses and hanging from the spokes of broken bicycle wheels. In the darkness when the silence was so thick that I thought I could feel the snow settling in the gutters and attic windows and in the elbows of trees, could almost see it nestling about the tops of telephone poles and magnolias and covering walls and fences with just the slightest hump, in those nights I would lie on my mattress listening for the creaking of the floorboards overhead and watching for the sudden appearance of your fine square shoulders at the top of the cellar stairs. I could see you standing there, gazing at me among the maze of yellow and silver figures, and though you would say nothing, I'd know that you understood. You'd lead me upstairs and show me the daylight on the curtains and the azaleas beginning to bloom, and then together we would arrange my figures in boxes, load them into your car trunk and slowly drive back to my classroom. Neither of us would speak, though at intersections we might exchange a glance, and our faces would be set in thin, firm smiles. At the school you'd stand beside your car and watch as I backed through the swinging doors, the boxes stacked in my arms higher than my eyes, and strode down the silent halls. My class would be waiting, of course, just as I had left them. And I'd resume the lesson exactly where I had ended it, would complete an interrupted sentence or discover on the board some half explicated proof. And with each step of my explanation I'd lift a shining figure and place it in the careful fingers of my students, and at last they would know the palpable forms of thought.

But sometimes I was troubled, Hazel. What if the classroom

were empty? I saw myself standing with the cold boxes in my arms gazing about me at the silent room.

Whenever I started thinking about these things, I would forget to warm my hands. I couldn't work in gloves, and though the cellar was warm enough to keep me comfortable in my down blanket, towels, and cap, the exposed skin of my hands always began to grow stiff and numb after only a few minutes. Whenever this happened I found myself cutting sections of wire imprecisely or occasionally breaking a whole side or angle when it was almost complete. I had to force myself to stop working, to lean back and hold my hands before the heat duct until my fingers began to itch with blood again.

At first this occasional clumsiness was not intolerable to me. As I imagined explaining to my students, space is patient. It waits. But then one day after I had been working for several hours on a pair of adjacent, mirror-image pentadecahedrons—I say several hours, but in reality, Hazel, it may have only been minutes, or it may have been weeks—my fingers, grown quite stiff with the cold, slipped from one of the vertices and broke through two horizontal parallels. Before I realized what was happening I was on my feet, trembling, waving the broken figure before me in the air. My students were shocked. I wanted to reassure them but somehow could not speak. And how strange they looked. Harelips, turgid pustules on cheeks and chins, snot encrusted septums, glabrous bellies that oozed over brass buckles, vermin infested pudenda, great strawberry marks over foreheads and eyes, slewed feet, scaley arms, brown teeth, denim crotches fat with priapic bloat. I leaned forward and took an obese student's nose between two fingers. It collapsed with a faint pop. They were so fragile. I bent down and pushed my hands into the soft surface of the mattress. And not beautiful at all. I ripped out two fistfuls of stuffing and threw the polyfoam particles up into the air. They drifted down over the bodies of my students. No, my students were clearly not beautiful. I picked up a can of nails and hurled it at them, but they did not move. And were they crying? I swung my fists at them, pulled down boxes and surfboards onto them, crushed them under my feet. They were everywhere, on every flat surface, sniffling at me from the walls, tumbling from fruit crates and bicycle wheels. A length of wood fell and struck my head, but I didn't stop. I threw books and plates, tore a section of pipe loose from a hammock stand and beat the stereo with it. I caught a fat jowl with my toe and tore it free. I planted my heel into kidneys and groin, flattened chests, ripped limbs and gouged eyes, and still they were crying.

I must have passed out finally, for I can't remember stopping. I only remember waking up on the concrete floor, my head pounding and my shoulders convulsing with the cold. The temperature in the room seemed to have dropped thirty degrees. I blinked my eyes, looked about me. The cellar was a shambles. Records were smashed. Table legs protruded from chair seats and picture frames. Book boxes were torn open and their contents spread across the floor.

I pulled my comforter back around my chest and started toward the heat duct. Then I saw the window. A two-by-four jutted from the broken glass. Snow poured in over the plank and formed a great mound on the basement floor. Where the drift had caved in above the top of the window I could see an oval section of gray sky. Wind came down this trough like an icy spike.

I scrambled to my feet and began tossing the snow back through the opening, at first with my hands and then with box lids and a rusted shovel blade. But it was no use. The more snow I forced out, the more I dislodged. Each time I bent for another load, my hands were covered with a cascade of ice.

Finally, I shoved a piece of cardboard into the opening and, rummaging through the piles of trash, found two irregularly cut pieces of plywood and a scrap of one-by-twelve. I formed them into as tight a cover as possible and, with a brick and some odd nails, fastened them over the window. There was nothing to do with the snow on the floor but brush it to one side and let it stay.

Then I received a shock. After clearing a path through the clutter and warming my hands in the air from the duct and breathing deeply to relax my lungs and heart, I began to look for my figures. They lay flattened and smashed in the rubble around the floor. I shook my head slowly and let my eyes fall onto the surface of the workbench. Lying across it was a coil of nickel-plated wire stretched and twisted to form a scalene triangle. Beside this were the cracked, mirror-image pentadecahedrons. These objects had somehow escaped my rampage. I stared at them in the circle of light from the bulb overhead. They seemed very distant from me now, as far removed as the dull memory of the scaffold itself, and yet they shone too. How had they survived? I ran my fingers hesitantly over their surfaces, touched the cracked joints, timorously stroked their angles and curves.

Then, for the first time, Hazel, I understood what space could become for me. I realized what my figures had always been trying to mean, and that now when you saw them you would understand, too. I began to limber my fingers in the warm air. I would build again, only now I would not restrict myself to discrete and familiar forms. I would let possibility devour space. I envisioned two-dimensional cones, thirteen-sided dodecahedrons, involuted ellipsoids, vanishing helices, spirals that shrunk and swelled, great networks of planar trisections, and impossible hyperboloids. I would fling thought into the realm of the scaffold itself.

I began working slowly and deliberately. No longer content with broom straw and bits of string, I began to scavenge conduit from the electrical circuits not in use. I tore helical coils from the decking of the divan and broke into the bedroom and cut the polyfoam and springs from the old boxsprings. I found two boxes of dry spackling and some putty knives in the attic and ripped down the linen curtains from the den. I melted the plastic shower curtain and trash receptacles in the oven, sawed the bookshelves into identical squares, cut the ends from all the extension and lamp cords and took up the strip flooring from the hall.

Soon the workbench was surrounded by mounds of materials. I built three equilateral pyramids, each over three feet high, and connected their vertices with coils of conduit and framing wire. With fabric, mucilage, and enamel I enclosed the sides and from one of these surfaces began a biplanar curve of masonite and Christmas styrofoam. I have no idea how long I worked. I wasn't sure any more if the kitchen clock still ran or how many days passed between my trips upstairs. Of course, I could have brought the clock downstairs, but in truth, Hazel, the thought never crossed my mind. I only know that at least twice, and surely more often than that, in the middle of my work I dozed off, my fingers still clutching coldly the rods and wires of my forms. Then in time I would reawaken, my mind as clear and quick as if I had only blinked my eyes, and, even if I had passed out halfway through some long and fluid operation, I would resume work as though I had never paused at all.

I hadn't forgotten you, Hazel, though as I worked now you weren't so clearly in my mind. I trussed up and glued strips of oak flooring into great polyhedrons and nailed each completed figure to a succession of others, all trailing over garden tools and stacks of broken crates and around support columns, and while I cut and measured and trimmed and bent, I always knew that you were there and that if I were to dig my way out of the house and somehow plow my walk clear again, I would still find your blood-brown hair whipping about your neck in the empty air. No, I hadn't forgotten you. What else did I measure in every length of pipe and straw and oak but your strong straight arms, and what but the diving curve of your spine had I found in every cone? Perhaps you had ceased to be a face for me, but this only means you were dispersed, not gone. You were the heat blowing against my cheek, the hot breath that drove the numbness from my hands, the light in which my figures shone.

And Hazel, how they shone. I rarely stood back from them now for they had twisted too deeply into my organs. I felt the sharp cusps of trapeziums puncturing my liver, felt my heart the vertex of a vast spreading cone, saw spirals radiating from my kidneys and a great convoluted icosahedron swelling from my groin. If I stood, I experienced a tightening of lines in my bowels and a weight like huge stone prismoids on my shoulders and lungs. The sensation was extraordinary. I developed the habit of relieving my bladder while seated, letting the urine find its smoking way through the dust and clutter. For a time I kept eating the canned peaches and dried toast we had hoarded in the kitchen cabinets, but eventually I forgot to eat at all. Soon my bladder and bowels required less attention. My eyes occasionally blurred, but otherwise I worked efficiently. I continued like this for months, I suppose. And all the while the linen and conduit and springs and wire and wood and straw and spackling and paint snaked upwards in planes and joints and gracefully ascending curves, filling every space, encircling the light, twisting among the crates and rubble around me.

Hazel, Hazel, Hazel! The shapes I made. You will never believe the shapes. Shapes human thought has never known. Shapes without names, Hazel. Curves that break and bend and disappear. Triangles from rectangles from gnomons from frustums from spirals from lines. Everything a creation of all others. Shapes, Hazel, forms. Perfection. Ah, if only you had seen.

Then one day I woke up with my head light and empty, my forehead resting on my crossed arms in the circular glow from the bulb overhead. My nostrils were damp with the sweetness of enamel and modeler's dope, and I had a sense of something familiar. I blinked. From somewhere light was leaking into the cellar. I stood slowly. I had forgotten how silver daylight could be. I stepped over boxes, a garden rake, edged around a smashed stereo speaker, and threaded myself between a polyfoam pentagram and two curving quadrilaterals until I stood before the boarded window. The one-by-twelve had come loose, and through the ragged seam between the plywood scraps, light projected a curiously phosphorescent spur onto my chest. I put my palm up to the opening. Warmth.

I worked my way back through my figures and climbed up the stairs. The living room and den seemed very different with daylight coming through the windows. I stepped carefully over the exposed floor joists in the hall and opened the front door. Ice hung in dripping spikes from the drains and tree limbs, and two small piles of snow stood on the lawn.

Wet snow was packed against the bottom of the screen, so I had to push against the aluminum edge with my shoulder until finally, with a great slosh, it came. I stepped out into the sun, paced up and down the walk with the warm air in my nose and throat. From somewhere I could hear a child sneezing. Down the block a neighbor stood over her spaniel as he defecated under a shrub. She waved, I think, shouted something about the thaw. I smiled.

In the mailbox I found some damp mail. Two bills, a statement from the bank, an old issue of *Time*, and, of course, the letter from you.

I sat down on the steps, gazed at the letters, and thought how odd daylight could make you feel and wondered how long before the azaleas would bloom.

I apologize to you, Hazel, for never opening your letter. You know I never meant to be rude. It was just that, sitting there, I had been unable to avoid staring out over the walk, and as I did, the mail slipped from my hand and dropped into the snow and my legs straightened and I pushed myself back to my feet and stumbled back inside. The bedroom door was still boarded and the living room was not very neat, but I could not help but be impressed with how much space there was in these rooms and with all the things that could fill such a space. I opened some windows in the kitchen, pulled out some drawers, and propped the back door to let a breeze come through. A wasp flew in the front door, inspected the clutter, then slouched out again. My first wasp of the year, Hazel. I cooked a steak that I found in the freezer and a mealy potato that had been preserved by the cold (I had to cut off the little tubers) and a box of frozen asparagus and sliced the edible portion of a bruised, softening apple. Then I strolled back outside and, leaning against the doorjamb, ate slowly with the warm breeze on my cheeks and watched the tree branches turning fuchsia as the sun went down.

For what I had seen as I sat on the edge of the steps with your letter in my hand and the melting snow seeping into my shoes and my eyes moving out across the sprouting grass and the puddles and the street—what I had seen was that the walk was empty, the air only empty air now, your blood-brown hair was gone. And I chewed my potato and cut my steak and felt my eyes grow hot and sucked my apple and felt my lips getting dry and pushed my asparagus between my teeth with my tongue until at last, when I could not eat any longer, I turned back inside and slipped down the cellar steps a last time, but this time left the door open behind me, thinking that after all it was only a short distance up the stairs into the living room, the empty living room. And there in the cellar before me, in the pale glow from the one bulb, amid the clutter of ripped pages and smashed records and broken frames, there they stood, the shining involutions of piecemeal things, but as strange and unthinkable as space itself, and as impalpable as love or time.

And, Hazel, they are beautiful.

PARADISE LOST

Begone wench of these once-seeing eyes, Beelzebub's whore, rail no more this Night's solitary night, depart! And would Paget play pander now and fetch me another? Chaste Urania waits in the garden, but 'twill be a cold Night's morn and no Kathy, good Kathy, to lead me by the hand.

My wife has started to rot.

"Ugh, Daddy, Mommy's titty fell off in the bran flakes!"

This is no cause for alarm. As I've told our daughter, Gloria, all life is compounded of mire and degenerates perpetually: necrobiosis is continual, in our bodies live the creatures that will eat us. But Gloria is eleven and finds biology confusing.

"Mommy, you smell like a fart."

"Is this a child at our breakfast table, Milton?" Agnes retrieves her nipple, cinches her bathrobe, and leaves for the beauty parlor in a trail of gray ash. "While I'm away, be a dear and brutalize the little beast for me."

I chew my sweetroll. "Autolysis is a natural process, Gloria. Everything changes, even mothers."

"Cow shit," she replies.

Every morning I shake Agnes' fetor from my houndstooth coat and drive past the nation's corps—Uni, Citi, Ameri, Bank—to the office tower where I used to drink quite a lot of coffee but now make bombs. I ride the elevator to the four-thousandth floor and greet Ms. Daltrey, the employee, who quits.

"I'm taking the elevator, I'm riding all the way to the ground,

17

I'm walking right out of this building. Everyone will remember me as the amazing woman who is gone."

"Later," I reply.

My office fills me with calm. From my window I can see the same ciphers rearrange themselves into the same configurations along the same crosswalks at the same hours every day. The Plexiglas window pane is an inch thick and I am told I can throw my desk at it without leaving a crack. The only sounds are the rrrrrrslck, rrrrrrslck of the copy machine, the faint rattle of computer keyboards, and Mr. Hamilton, my lawyer, thrashing the auditor in the hall across the way. I spread a large map of the city onto my desk and buzz Ms. Daltrey.

"Nobody works here. What do we produce? Morale in this office is very low. Cream?" she asks and places the forty-cup percolator on my typing table.

"Call Commissioner Correzano and tell him I'll need a roll of nichrome wire, insulated. No, black, thanks."

Making bombs adds substance to your character. You walk straighter, look police dogs in the eye. I used to be a man of fashion living whole lifetimes in a single night. At the office in the morning no one recognized me. Now I am capable of vast destruction and this gives me pause. I read memos and street signs cautiously. People become attentive when I speak in my measured tones. I am a grave man and have learned to live more deliberately than time.

"Money," Correzano announces as he lurches through my doorway.

I nod and peel two leg wires from the roll he hands me. "I once met a tall man who had money. He wore a blue suit and smiled a lot. I remember thinking: there's something about him, and wondered was he religious. Later I realized, no, he's rich."

"All those people out there." The sweep of Correzano's arm takes in my window, two pigeons, a news helicopter, the distant TASHITO softwares sign partial power-failure has rendered obscene, and the fifty-thousandth floor of the adjacent General-corp Building in a window of which two perspiring tax consultants arm wrestle one another on a shiny desk. "Their lives stagnated, their vitality gone, deprived of opportunity, force, direction."

I attach the wires to a blue Dupont detonator, lock the cap in a file drawer, and touch the loose ends to my power cell. BAMP! My office staff comes running to investigate. "An adventure!" Correzano bolts the door.

"How to return their lives to them?" he asks. "How to extend the power to create, to realize the new?"

"Absolute otherness."

"A color TV."

I inspect the file drawer. "Now that ethylenedianimedinitrate has gotten so scarce, I sometimes feel like an electrician. But I guess every job has its drawbacks."

Correzano helps me empty the coffee percolator into the toilet. "Nothing is immortal, Milton," he giggles. "Not even concrete and steel."

I smile. "Money is the wave of the future."

"Bombs keep it flowing."

We pick up the carton of ANFO and start out the door.

"While I'm away, Ms. Daltrey, try very hard to be still."

Later when I return there is a message for me to phone Agnes at the beauty parlor. She asks me will I pick her up on my way home. Her skin has been freshly painted and she's afraid driving will cause her to sweat.

"I am a short blond college sophomore with a Southern accent and an intense interest in sexual novelty," she tells me.

"I don't hear the accent."

"Bobby isn't finished yet."

I find her waiting beneath the huge and mysterious sign that fills my heart with dread. She's wearing an extraordinarily leggy skirt, and though there's still not much accent, her hair is the strawberry shade that's my favorite. We stop twice to perform panting acrobatics in the back seat before arriving home.

Gloria meets us at the door. "Mommy called. She says dishwater blond, not strawberry. Can I ride?"

I apologize for my mistake; seems this one really is a college sophomore, but from southern Pennsylvania. We drop her at a bus stop and return to the beauty parlor. Agnes is still waiting but her nose has come loose and little piles of greasy pumice have begun to form on her shoulders and breast.

"Nothin' lasts, nothin' a-tall," Agnes sobs.

"I thought Bobby promised you a permanent."

"Oooooo, Daddy, Mommy's got a worm in her hair!"

"Milton, sugah, would you put the awfspring in the trunk, please?"

I remove Gloria, "No kicking," and we drive home without a word. When I stop the car, Agnes sighs.

"Bobby says it costs a heap o' money to make somethin' permanent."

"Ewk! Ewk!" Gloria says. Thunk. Thunk. Thunk.

I shift in my seat. "Maybe first we should see a doctor."

"How long since you took her out for dinner, Mr. Milton? Just the two of you." The doctor's hair is wavy, gray. For emphasis he raps the desk with the ear clamps of his stethoscope, sinks deeper into his leather chair. "A place with a view, on the river front, or one of those turning restaurants up high. Soft light, good wine, a little flamenco guitar." He makes a strumming motion with his hand. "I recommend the broiled sea bass in fruit sauce."

"You don't understand," Agnes begins.

I lean forward. "She's going bad, sour. Look here." I pinch a swatch of crumbly corium from Agnes' biceps, hold it to the doctor's nostrils.

"Phew!" He laughs. "Well, we can't stay twenty years old forever, can we now, Mrs. Milton?"

"My beautician says—"

"What is youth? Where is it when it's gone?" He waves his hand in the air, smiles broadly. "How long since the two of you had a good screw?"

"Doctor, I'm not his *secretary*!"

"Sunday night I nibbled her earlobe and it fell off."

The doctor chuckles, leans toward us. "Ever had sex after a funeral?"

Agnes begins to cry. "Something is happening to me!"

"Now, now," he chides. "You aren't sick; you're just dying."

Agnes runs from the office.

"But...but her body—"

With a faint woosh of air the doctor descends still deeper into the leather pleats. "Advice, Mr. Milton, just between us men." He winks. "Enjoy it."

On the six o'clock news Correzano is sterling. "Terror! Disruption! An infection in the tissue of national life. Today Unicorp, tomorrow my office, your home. And yet everywhere officials demand a little more time, a little more time." The camera shots are beautiful, soft ocher clouds where concrete used to be. Just over Correzano's shoulder is a showroom window filled with color TV's. The commentator interviews a dusty police captain. An ambulance shrieks away.

"Bobby say permanent take care everything." Tonight Agnes is a geisha who at two this afternoon was fourteen but since has begun to show her age.

"What style?" I ask.

"We choose," she replies plucking her shamisen and beginning to hum.

The picture returns to the studio where a spokesman for Unicorp has begun to discuss the economic effects of the disaster. "...not just management. Really, we have to speak of citywide consequences, perhaps statewide. There is no such thing as mere company loss."

The humming seems to have made Agnes' effluvia more noxious than usual. I pinch my nose. "Where's Gloria?"

Agnes frowns. "In it room, I sup-hose. Royster boys here."

Gloria's door is locked. I hear a snicker, the creee of bed springs. I knock softly.

"What do YOU want?" A shirtless teenage boy peers at me through the crack.

"You fellas having a nice time? Like something to drink? Want to watch TV?"

He rolls his eyes. "Gloria warned us you'd snoop."

The room is too dark to make out more than the rolling motion of vague shapes. Correzano's voice rises momentarily from the den. "...birthpangs, irresistible change..."

"Gloria all right?"

The boy winks back. "The best we've ever had, Mr. Milton."
The door closes and I hear laughter, some coughing, a moan,
"Noooo..."

When I return to the den Agnes is regluing a broken fingernail.
"Bobby say no major work require. Basic struc-ture...," she
smooths her gown on her hips, "velly strong."

The news is ending and I see the cityscape moving slowly across
the screen. Correzano's face momentarily reappears. "...look for
culprits, sure! Everyone wants to root out the 'criminal element,'
but where, Gentlemen, I ask where is the man who wants to know
the cause?"

"...conspiracy, Commissioner?"

Correzano leans close to the camera, seems about to wink at me
but resists. "Forces, Gentlemen. We are being controlled."

I stand a moment watching the commentator eat his micro-
phone before a pile of rubble as firemen wander by in search of
someone with a plan. Agnes has picked up her shamisen and is
humming again.

"Ask Bobby how much," I say.

This morning my office is as cool as wind in trees. I stand in
each of the four corners, my feet buried to the ankles in umber
pile, and wonder if a people has a mind. From my window I watch
the ciphers on opposite curbs flow forward and interpenetrate,
specks of blackness bunching and thinning, and decide this is
motion but not change. Individuality exists at a height but on the
pavement, within the group life, it is difficult to know whether the
sportspage before my face is held in my fist or another man's. So
when Ms. Daltrey steps out of her dress I am a trifle long gazing at
her knees wondering why they aren't mine.

"Mistake," I say.

"Sometimes, Mr. Milton, I think you're losing interest in your
work."

"Family problems," I offer, but it is a weak attempt.

"We're not insensitive to the personal element around here
but, you understand, business is business." She eyes my coffee
mug longer than is polite then exits with a chilly flip of her head.

When Correzano arrives he is depressed. "We alter the features, Milton, lift the face, but there's no heart in it."

I nod. "It's hard living in the future."

"You know what really makes me happy these days?"

"Pills?"

"Bribery." He sinks into the lounge chair beside my desk, gazes out the window. His pupils are black bugs in saffron puddles. "Last week I arranged for Allicorp to pay Maxicorp two hundred grand so Maxicorp's man in Cincinnati could wash it through labor and make a contribution to Eastern Philanthropies which a girl of mine in records there could divert to a private account I draw on to buy off the local organization in Hampton Heights so they'll threaten to riot two days before the mayoral election. But you know what I did?"

I'm silent, watching.

"Went to church."

Through the doorway I hear the gurgle of the percolator, the titter of scandal, the rattytattytatty of a computer printer creating the world.

"The sanctuary was empty. I piled all the bills on the altar, then I got the giggles real bad. For a long time I couldn't leave, just sat there giggling."

"A man ought to be either good or happy," I say. "Seems unfair being neither one."

Correzano looks at me. "Who's the enemy, Milton?"

I begin to thumb my copy of Stoffel's *Homemade Bombs*. "Principles are for dead people, Correzano. Don't look for principles."

"Women are reality, Mr. Milton. You, me, what are we? Did we ever launch a ship, cause a war, beget a messiah, inspire a masterpiece?" He is slender and so neat his hair looks glazed. "If they pass away, there is nothing—NOTHING—left."

"I am not a rich man."

"Do you know what Tillich called the great turning point in his life? When he asked himself, 'Paul, how come there's anything at all?' " Bobby leans closer. His breath is cool and sweet as cherry pop. "That's the question I'm asking you, Mr. Milton. How much is it worth to you that there's anything at all?"

"$500.00."

He stiffens, draws his whole weight up into his chest. "Excuse me, I mistook you for a serious man."

"Then you set a figure."

"The figure, Mr. Milton, is fine. The decimal is an insult."

"Look, my wife is becoming a corpse."

"Who isn't?"

I fix him with my eyes. "I don't know. You tell me. Who isn't?"

Bobby smiles. "There are nights, you've known them, when it is the first night all over again, and think of the first night. It hardly moves, a photograph, complete—the hand caught rising to brush away a single hair, motion forever suspended, Keats' pursuing Greeks. Some people grow young. Wine is renewed and enlivened with years. Where is that line between ripeness and corruption? A boundary so slender it appears to be the mere meeting of the two. Ah, but if we could only capture it, that timeless strand of living time—"

"$5,000.00."

His face rushes down into my face, his brows arch like bridges as they explode. "I am speaking of immortality, Mr. Milton! Of life!" He spins on his heel and is out of the room before he hisses back, "Nothing *has* to change."

Morning of the Night, as the dank zephyr bestirs the house, and soon will be day, then ev'n of the Night and night of the Night once again, in which all times and seasons celestial effluence increase doth shine but confusedly, luming darkness palpable, Stygian heart, blindness doubly blinded as another time she comes, whether from perdition delinquent to wrong spouse Lucifer's sheets and me, or Heav'n lent, gift of renewed youth and sight, I know not, nor ever will, only that as she kneels my anger flees leaving me undefended, old fool atremble in his dotage, the

toy of blood's storm and my neighbor's derision, deprived even of
those eyes I might have plucked out would to do so have saved me
this thralldom to blinding light that will not be obscured. And
now Paget would fetch me another. Hah! Will corporeal heart be
never so chastened that vain desire cannot 'twine its sleek shape
round the tubers of Conscience, Holy Fruit corrupt, and by vile
hint of bliss more sharply spiced than peace of Soul with
Heavenly Reason endued, dim the Vital Lamp, Beam eclipse,
Word blot out, and desert me in this shadow of hell-flame and
blood lechery, staked, lashed, beaten by memory, my divine
image imbruted, as the frosty breeze whips these old shins, chills
my slow-waking thoughts, and with the stillness of Night's morn
recalls my fear that you, O Holy Mistress, jealous of your place
and in flight from yon harlot's vulgar sheen, that this day you
will not breathe your breath into me. Begone, Mary! Would not
stay when I and duty bade you, now leave your husband this
Night his only peace. Dark, dark, dark. I know morning by the
lark's music and the rattle of the rag-picker's cart, by the ache of
stiff bones, by the return of heroic numbers to be sung.

　　Life is complicated. I'm lying in bed listening to the hum of
insects above Agnes' pillow and trying to finish this dream about a
cormorant sitting in a fruit tree beside a river when my shoulder
starts to itch. I slap at it and get a muffled bzzzzup! and some juice
on my palm. One of Agnes' flies, but on me. Which makes me
uneasy, just like the rim of mildew on my file drawer and the rust
stain in my carpet or the hint of canker from the shower curtain
and, on my finger, these tiny bubbles like zits but inflamed. And
passing the office manager's computer this morning I feel an urge
to make it tell me a lie, and when I say "Yes" to Ms. Daltrey's
question would I like to buy into the office pool on the market
analyst clinging to the window ledge of the Petrocorp Building
across the way, I can't tell if my response is mere courtesy, habit,
noise, or possibly an accidental appearance of the truth.
　　She is aware of my confusion and has obviously prepared for it.

"I would have liked to handle this between ourselves, Mr. Milton, but..." Lifting an eyelid and strutting to the door, she motions into the hall.

"Sorry," she says back to me. Not insincerely, I think.

"What is it, Miltie boy? Pineal gland? Midlife?"

"And we believed in you so."

"Hey, kid, this is an upbeat place. We're producers—"

"—fighters—"

'—winners."

"We're SEXY!!!"

Mr. Hamilton stands before my desk, arms crossed over his chest, his lavender boxing trunks and shiny Everlast headgear flashing at me like a warning. Behind him a dozen junior partners from his firm shoulder each other nervously, their pinstripes dilating with every leap of my arteries, their hands hanging like meatloaves from their navy blue sleeves. The obese receptionist waddles toward me in her powder-pink teddy and plops an enormous breast on my arm. The auditor sways, bloody and bleary-eyed, between two sales managers and leers up into my face. Over everything I hear the gurgling of the percolator and an occasional shriek from the market analyst who now has worked his way back onto the ledge and is gesticulating at someone half a million feet below him on the ground.

"A period of personal growth," I say. "A time for reflection. Who knows? I may be on the threshold of a surge."

"Six weeks and not one appearance on the squash court."

"Not a single hand of interoffice blackjack—"

"Not even a round of computer bingo!"

"And poor, poooor Ms. Daltrey..."

Mr. Hamilton jabs a begloved thumb at my head. "We're talking about sap, Milton, pizzazz. This isn't any country for old men."

"The world has become mysterious," I say. "The present is not itself anymore. We must try very hard to be quiet."

"He's calling this a crisis!" someone cries.

"...distressing lack of idealism."

Mr. Hamilton leans toward me. "Milton, are you losing faith in us?"

"Faith?"

"Where would we be today if everybody thought before doing their jobs?"

"Sometimes I look out my window and realize the world is a vast organism. There is a marvelous coherence down on the street, but seeing it requires a great height. Only the weightiest souls, the gravest minds can overcome fashion. Very soon everything will be new." I can feel the sweat seeping through my coat sleeves. The room has grown very still. "It's not always so clear, you know . . . just what a person ought to do."

The auditor giggles. The meatloaves twitch. Suddenly the receptionist's gelatinous embonpoint swoops down into my face. "Mr. Milton! Are you falling in love with your wife?"

And there's no point in responding because already I've noticed the ripple in the row of pinstripes, the oncoming wave, and now just above the mounds of pink corpulence pressing against my nose I can see the cylinder rise up as silver and shiny as a brightly polished engine of war. "You wouldn't," I say.

Ms. Daltrey glares over at me. "No employee likes to feel unappreciated, Mr. Milton."

"I'll buy three chances in the office lottery. I'll visit the company weightroom—"

But it's too late. I feel the thick pinstriped fingers pressing my shoulders to the desk, a letter opener shoved in between my teeth, my mouth prized open as the cylinder is raised above my head and the scalding black bean-liquor is poured down my throat.

"Aaaargh!" I say.

"Gurgle, gurgle," the percolator replies.

"Aieeeeeeeeeeeeeeeeeeeee," calls the market analyst as he plummets to the earth.

And they are right. Long after the last orgasms have faded from the secretarial pool I sit twisting a nichrome fuse into a spiral about my thumb. The thud and grunt of jabs to the body no longer sound from the auditor's office and out my window the ciphers have disappeared from the street. I can see the lights winking off in the Petrocorp Building, vice presidents repositioning ties and brassieres, packing up backgammon boards, changing from sneakers to wingtips and heels again. Everyone is returning home for a well-deserved night of boredom, alcohol, Valium, sleep. The city has begun to look disturbingly vulnerable, and I realize only the future remains pure now. The future and Correzano.

"I'm going to find it, Milton."

"It?"

He thumps his solar plexus. "The heart. No more piddling with inessentials. The question is: what's the enemy of money?"

I steer the car into an alley beneath a fire escape and peer through the windshield at the street, a line of taxis waiting by the curb, two bag ladies screeching at each other beside a traffic light. "How do you know when you're dead, Correzano?"

He looks at me a long time before answering. "Fuzzy pictures," he finally says.

"Like a bad tube?"

"Fuzzy smells, too."

"But how come these people will begin to behave so strangely when in," I check my watch, "seven seconds the five-hundredth floor of the Telecorp Building over there removes itself to the street?"

It does; they do.

"Fuzzy pictures?" I ask.

Correzano begins to laugh and perspire. "At the end of a movie I have to leave. At the end of a play the curtain falls. At the end of a concert I applaud. Money buys occasions. No one ever has enough of it. But what if after an hour and a half the lights come on and some joker yells, 'To be continued next week'?"

I gaze out the window at an elderly man clinging to a decapitated parking meter as his cortex drips from a saucer-sized dent above his nose.

"People are prepared for things to end," Correzano adds. "They never expect them just to stop." We can hear the first sirens in the distance.

"You got any pancake in the glove compartment?" I ask. "Your forehead's shiny."

Correzano pats me on the knee. "Death's a mystery, Milton. Comes to all of us. Sometimes asking questions doesn't help." We steer past the flattened taxis and bag ladies into a street of limbs, organs, screams, rubble. Policemen are running about uselessly. To my right I notice a labrador retriever poking its muzzle under a collapsed awning and wagging its tail. "Up and out now," I say pointing toward the news van. "Time's money."

Correzano grins back at me. "And the enemy?"

"Whatever resists time."

"Exactly," he says starting to sprint toward the cameras. "The enemy is the heart."

"$5,000,000,000.00!!!!!!!!!!!!!!!!!!!!!!!!!!!!!!!!!!!!!?????"

"Let's speak frankly, Mr. Milton. You fucked up. I won't waste time with explanations. Maybe it was something your wife ate — an undisciplined diet can account for a lot. But it's enough that you had the chance to fuck up and you did. Now you come to Bobby asking him to make everything right again, and, believe me, I'd like to, I'd like to. But there's more involved here than changing plugs and points. A process has to be reversed. There are principles. That means an entire reconception." He leans forward. "We're not talking about architecture, Mr. Milton. We're talking about grace."

"A-a miracle?" I ask.

Bobby fixes me with his eyes. "Anything that lasts is a miracle."

Home.

"Pear-haps my dancing make you deezy, senor? Pear-haps I come down these table and we look at the peektures, si?"

For the third night this week Agnes is Carmen, which is okay except that the perpetual clanging of ankle bells and finger cymbals has begun to give me a headache. The kitchen table is littered with Bobby's catalogs, all the latest models, over seventy thousand

styles to choose from. I chew my potato and stare through Agnes'
prancing feet at the news commentator who I'm beginning to
think may be dangerous.

"...not just haphazard terrorism, commissioner, then should
we speak of *meaningful* terrorism?"

"Page twenty-seex. Ease called Mother's Cherry Tart. You
like?" Agnes places her heel in the butter dish and turns the pages
of the uppermost catalog with her large toe. "The skeen ease
maybe too pink? The hair ease too blund?"

"Gloria eaten yet?"

Clang! Clang! Brrring! "Who ees these Gloria? I scratch her
eyes out. I keel her. Hi-yeeeee!"

"Our daughter."

"Oh, si, the servant child? She ease down in the cellar. I geeve
her the old clothes to play weeth."

"...anarchy, nihilism, international hooligans—just words,"
Correzano exclaims. "What's important is to sense a direction..." His lip has begun to quiver.

I flip the page. "It doesn't seem to be quite you."

"These 'who am I' ease not the interesting question. I am
nahthing. I am many pear-sons."

"But in order to decide—"

"I am your lahving wife, senor. I weel place a rose between my
teeth for your entertainment. I weel pear-form an unnatural act.
I weel be whatever your heart desires. Page thirty-two. Sweet
Georgia Brown."

The catalog photo is of a six-two mulatto with enormous
haunches and carnivorous mouth. She is sucking a tangerine lol-
lipop and fondling herself. The skin sample feels disquietingly
supple. "Maybe we shouldn't rush into this. There's always
homeostasis. Er...ah...I'm having some difficulty with the
price."

"...seem to be saying, commissioner, that the present situa-
tion is, in a manner of speaking, perfectly nat—"

Agnes kicks the pot roast into the TV screen. "My teeth, they
are rotten! My hair, eet ease falling out! I theenk you weesh to be

reed of me. I theenk you desire a yahnger woman. I theenk you are a fucking ass-hole."

"Waaaaaaaah!" Gloria marches into the kitchen wearing Agnes' black garters, panties, cutaway brassiere, and leather knee boots. "I want a period," she cries.

"Patience," I say.

"I want boobies. I want tampons. I wanna be knocked up."

"Feed the peegs," Agnes says.

"Daddy, Tommy Royster paid me three dollars to tie him to a mattress. Why is Mommy so noisy?"

Agnes is dancing the Tarantella. Her foot comes loose with a little pop and bounces off the wall. "Senor, eenstruct the servant child to geeve to me my ankle."

"P.U.!" Gloria cries. "It's all buggy!"

"Sometimes children have to make sacrifices for their parents," I say.

"Oh Daddy, you're so silly. Nobody believes that anymore." Gloria crawls up into my lap, gives me a hug. "How long before we can put Mommy in the dirt?"

"Hi-yeeeee!" a knife sails past Gloria's ear.

"Middle-aged housewife!" she screeches and runs to her bedroom. "I'm gonna call a lawyer."

"... twisting my ... my words ..."

"Not at all, commissioner, but if nature is more than a figure of speech ..."

Through the carrots and gravy I can see the sweat glistening on Correzano's forehead.

"Senor Bobby's price, eet ease very high?"

"Metaphysical."

Agnes lowers her face to mine. Her breath smells like Sangria. "My hossband, you know how much these mean to me."

"How much?"

She looks back at me a long minute, then, "Eet ease my life."

Which doesn't sound quite right, but I'm not sure just why. An aspirin commercial has taken over the screen, and I rush to the phone to call Correzano. When I return, Agnes has taken off her wig, lashes, prosthesis, teeth, nails, shoulder pads, corset, contacts, jewelry, lipstick, rouge, mascara, and is swatting flies with the newspaper. "I think we need to do something about Gloria," she says.

But I'm back at the office.

"I've made a discovery, Milton. Money is its own end."

"He ate you alive."

"You're still innocent. You haven't acquired the long vision. People are not real."

"Have you been reading the polls again?"

Correzano hangs his head. "I got lonely."

I stir the huge coffee mug that sits on the edge of my desk, take a taste. They've got me on a refill schedule, and somebody has figured out a way to wire my toilet bowl for grounds. My only hope is to sip slowly and try to outlast them. "The world's rotten, Correzano. You live in the future or you live in shit."

"The interviewer wasn't there."

"Half a million voters saw that interview. They have memories."

"AFL-CIO loves me, IBM loves me, NEA loves me, the National Rifle Association and B'nai B'rith love me, even the Quakers love me. Computers have memories. Voters have glands."

I slop my coffee on the carpet. Already I'm feeling restless. If I drink any more of this stuff, I'll start making decisions. "Don't fuck up, Correzano."

But he doesn't know me.

"History can be erased," he says.

"History can blow up in your face."

"Check the videotape. Try to find his name in the actors' guild or the broadcasters' association or the phone book. Drive by his street address; it's a vacant lot. The newspapers'll tell you they've never heard of him. If you read the transcript of the show you'll find—"

"I saw him."

"You saw a TV screen."

"I saw him."

"You saw what the camera showed you. You don't know what you saw."

"People are real!"

"Software is real, money is real, bombs are—"

I can't stand this. I open my file drawer, pull out a lamp timer and two blasting caps. "Let's get to work." But he doesn't budge. "I'm real."

Ms. Daltrey comes through the doorway wearing a champagne negligee, Converse tennies, handball glove, and carrying two cups of coffee. Correzano takes the cup she offers him, toasts me. "Today, Milton, time stands still." He slips an arm around Ms. Daltrey's waist. "Your friend and I... we have a date."

And my office has vanished. In its place is the wild jangling of caffeine, caffeine. I slash my way through the carpet with a penknife, beat back snarling cockroaches with my paperweight. I am famished for the dark flavor of cunnilingus, pillage, cruelty, blood. I blow up my file cabinet. I blow up my desk. I blow a hole in the elevator doors and throw Ms. Daltrey's computer into the shaft. Down on the street the ciphers rush frantically together, interpenetrate, explode, turn black, white, red, flatten into nothingness again, and I am writhing on the floor, pink foam clinging to my lips, grinding a fuse between my teeth, when the cleaning lady arrives.

"Outcha my way. Gots to clean. Ain't clean, somebody bitches. Somebody bitches, life's rotten. Life's rotten, who cares? Outcha my way. Nice shoes there." She taps the bottoms of my soles with her vacuum tube.

"Grrrrrrr," I say.

"Don't talk witcha mouth full," she says and yanks the fuse out of my jaw. "Ain't polite."

"Sorry," I choke, swallow. "Expensive, the shoes."

She's impressed. "Mind?" She spits on the hem of her dress, kneels and buffs the toes. "My face." She points at her reflection in the cordovan. "You ain't no muggist or raper?"

"Make bombs," I say.

"Man needs a hobby." She slaps at the rubble that was my desk
with her dust rag, dumps the trashcan next to the typing table into
the trashcan beside the john, lights a cigarette with the fourteen-
karat gold lighter she finds beneath a twisted file drawer, and
plops down into my chair. "You the guy been blowin' up everybody?"

"How'd you guess?"

"Cleanin' people know a lot. Who sneaks in early, who stays
late, who's stuffin' condoms down the stool, where you keep yer
dirty pictures, when you dump yer whiskey bottle in the burger
bag. Cleanin' crew knowed six months you's the bomber."

"Wife stinks."

She nods, "Same's my Ernie, 'fore he died. Enough to make
you want to blow up somethin'. But now I'm of two minds on it."

"Bad bones, bad skin, bad organs, bad breath," I say.

"Yeah, but my Ernie, wasn't much to him, y'know. He'd be
sittin' there readin' the funnies, and 'less you kicked him, you
wasn't sure he's anything at all. But stinkin' made him be there.
He'd come in the room, folks'd look up, say 'lo Ernie; he talked,
everybody'd listen." She chuckles. "Ol rascal. He got damn near
interesting there at the end."

"I'd like to live a dull life," I say.

"No help. Dyin' don't ignore so good. Livin' ain't so much,
though. Folks looked right through my Ernie when he was livin'.
But once he started to rot . . ." She winks at me. "Well, you smelt
my Ernie, you knowed him." She's gone.

And tonight the bedroom is so thick with flies the TV tube looks
cloudy. I lie beside Agnes in the dark stirring the buzzing air with
a newspaper, cotton swabs stuffed up my nostrils, as the commentator hums and hahs up to Correzano whose smile is as tantalizing
as the veil of truth. "Order?" Correzano asks. "In everything
there is order, but to see it, that takes courage, that takes genius.
No one needs to impose a shape on the crisis; we must gaze where
shape is emerging, where pattern enters history, where space
enters time. In short, we must catch the thugs!" I sit bolt upright
in bed. There is a frenzy of questions from the newsmen. Correzano has begun to leer at the screen. "I have some leads," he

says. "And a witness." Before the camera Ms. Daltrey stands and begins to unsnap her brassiere.

"A law, Mr. Milton, like supply and demand, what the market will bear, caveat emptor, but older, simpler, more natural. We're approaching the limits of money. No investment, no harvest, but money, you understand, cannot make things grow." Bobby raises an eyebrow, gazes over at me. "Some principles go deeper than money."

"She says it's her whole life."

"And nothing's worth more than that."

"But if it's priceless, then how—"

"Not priceless. Merely incalculable."

I watch him for a long moment, then he says:

"An eye for an eye, a tooth for a tooth. We can't set a figure, but we can make an exchange."

But this Elizabeth is his cousin, Paget says, and a hardy service-able wench, and the house needs a mistress, and half my age! and surely hath no mind fit for pleasing converse, though "John, you are scarce old and she nearly a quarter span and you a man of reputation and not poor" and an ungovernable libertine who even now in Heav'n's pure Light walks but confoundedly, as Sightless sightless as when seeing did saddle his mare of a morn-ing, God wot why, and rode out to debase his Maker's handiwork before a milk-white brow, dark hair atumble, eye, neck, shoul-ders so pale, so round, so warm beneath my palm that even now would return from hellfire to drag me down. Ah, Mary, wife of these eyes, how you wronged me, how I was wronged, wrong, we wronged, so, so wrong. . . . Here's a light doth scald, a flame will darken, Lucifer's own brilliance would itself consume. Is not a single display of womanish infirmity sufficient? Must I, like goatish David, procure young flesh to heat old bones? I would be a poet, not an old fool. A cold Night this day, and the vein in the hoarfrost runs slow. To lose the light in Smyrna or Chios, bare

feet upon sun-warmed rocks, the hiss of the Aegaeum in your
ear, nostrils swollen with dank salt.... Maeonides lost nothing.
But here as the stench of English winter comes apace and the
Bedlamite stillness of snow falls upon Jewin Street and seals a
man in blindness like a box, to lose light here is to lose a world.
Word, Word, what wouldst Thou have me see? I am Milton, one
who delights in the talk of sober minds, adores Right, hath spilt
his ink and light for Liberty (doing it will make thee go blind, they
said), knows the worth of friends, and can tell what Evil comes
from desiring overmuch of womankind. To the garden. Keep
silence, wait, listen, when the breath stirs sing. Ah, but the
Muses —were they not also women?

Gloria is waiting for me at the playground. When she climbs
into the car, I notice she isn't wearing her pants.

"I gave 'em to Tommy Royster. A souvenir." She stares out
the window. "Where are we going, Daddy?"

I steer onto the interstate. "Years before you were born,
Gloria, people were very boring. It was much easier then to sit
still. If a person asked a question, he got an answer that sounded
like an answer." We pass an army convoy, two junkyards, a
furniture factory on strike. As we start under a bridge a child in a
white sailor cap leans over the railing and lands a globule of spit on
our windshield eight inches from my nose. I have begun to sweat.
"Do you realize that this highway we're on is one big circle? The
same stretch of road goes into the city and out again, around it in
both directions. Even that exit over there is a spiral."

Gloria stares in the direction I am pointing. My daughter is
beginning for the first time to see the shape of things. "Wh-
where's Mommy?"

"Mommy is becoming...completely new."

"Mommy's nothing?"

"Mommy's everything." We turn off the access road and stop
the car in front of the strip center we both know, the huge blue
sign that fills my heart with wonder.

"Then we're alone now."

"In the modern world, Gloria, everyone is always alone."

She draws closer to me, places her hand lightly on my thigh, her face against my face. "Tommy Royster says he'll love me forever," she whispers.

Understanding is a form of deterioration. There are some things I'd prefer not to understand. I draw her to my chest. "There is no such thing as forever, dear."

Suddenly the door swings open and the car is invaded by shining white teeth, yellow hair glued to its scalp, eyes bluer than ice.

"What a lovely little girl," the face says.

"Yeccch!" Gloria vomits onto the floor mat.

I place my hand on her knee to steady her. "Gloria, dear, I want you to meet Bobby. Your new father."

And I fill my car trunk with ANFO, and I crawl over the corps of the city laying gleeful waste. I restore air, sky; I teach concrete to disappear. I am mightier than software, mightier than the three-piece suit, mightier than Mr. Hamilton and drugs and the tax consultants who diddle one another on shiny desks, mightier almost than coffee, here where the ciphers rush together, where Ms. Daltrey will do anything, anything, and where the auditor meets me as I step from the elevator and informs me with a giggle that I do not exist.

"Where's the pencil sharpener? Where's the percolator? Where's the office manager? Where's me?"

"Aren't."

The auditor's left arm is in a sling, and his face is a puffy mass of bandaids and shiners. If his eyes were any deeper inside his skull, you couldn't find them, but no mistaking that he's happy. "Absent. Vanished. Tee hee."

"But the receptionist alone weighed a thousand pounds!"

"We finished the audit. I can show you the printout. This company's been nothing for nearly three years."

The rooms are lovely. Windows breaking the bare expanse of white walls, sunlight strewn across the carpet, the lines where planes intersect, silence. It's as if time had been sucked out a heat vent. "I was substantial. I had a desk."

"Despite miraculously fluid cash flow, you were never a business. Mitsubishi and Sakurai consolidated their holdings in your original manufacturing concern four years ago and now constitute the controlling interest, and your marketing division was subcontracted to a local research group that has since gone public and contests its status as an entity. You continued to retain partial control over your chemical laboratories through a joint venture with Cropcorp Co-op, but last March they filed Chapter Eleven, and immediately all experiments became the property of a savings and loan institution in Utah that insists on remaining anonymous. There's a silent partner involved, but our research indicates that this is an arm of the Batista government in exile, which is not recognized. IBM has a piece of you, as do AT&T, Citicorp, Time, Dow, Holiday Inn Corp Incorp, and Schaeffer Ink Inc, but because of tax liabilities each investor lists its shares under names other than your own. Geico bought the video screens. Suzuki bought the receptionist. Technically you could be said to exist as long as certain civil suits are pending, but to say in the present circumstance that any institution holds any interest in *you* is to speak figuratively. Your attorneys put up a spirited resistance; you can be proud of them. However, I think you'll agree with me that this has been a triumph of the reality principle."

"B-but money..."

The auditor's mouth begins to twitch, his eyebrows to rise.

"Surely someone has made some money," I say.

He jerks down into a crouch, throws up his guard, and starts to hop around me on the balls of his feet. "You just try it. I outlasted Hamilton. I can lick you all. Come at me, come at me."

I gaze up at the ceiling. The emptiness in here is palpable. I can feel it buzzing in my teeth. "Don't exist," I repeat.

"Someone could write you a check, but the accounts don't exist. Neither do the authorized signatures. No checkbooks, no fountain pens, nothing to bear down on."

"What about the cleaning crew? Who bought the cleaning crew?"

"Computer company. Orange, peach, pear, plum. Can't quite recall..."

I look up and he's already punching the elevator button. "One word," he says. "Fruit. Name of the company. Tee hee."

Tee hee?

And that's when I know I'm about to discover something terrible and true. "Hey!" I dash for the opening, but the doors are pinching closed on his grinning face. Absent. Aren't. And I'm down the corridor and into the stairwell and leaping whole flights at a time, fifty floors, two hundred fifty, thinking between gasps that the sky is safe only if the ground is sure, five hundred floors and onto the sidewalk and sprinting curbward and into the street and the backseat of Correzano's idling car and speeding off down the block as my office takes flight in a hellish thunderstorm of concrete, dissolves, becomes nothing, air, an idea the future has chosen to ignore.

"It arrived in a vision," Correzano is saying. "A dream sprung of the heart, entire in a moment. I got up this morning, strode to the car, and knew that no matter which way I turned the wheel, I would eventually meet the enemy of money."

"All disappointments converge there." Ms. Daltrey unrolls a length of nichrome wire from a spool between her feet, holds her pocketknife across the insulation. "What's the best way to skin this fuse, Mr. Milton?"

This life is familiar; I've lived it before. I ease down into the seat, let my shoulders relax. "Split the leg wires first, then peel. Don't uncover the power source yet. Where exactly is this place?"

Correzano stares into the road; Ms. Daltrey concentrates on her hands. I realize their silence is inspiration and so watch the interstate pass slowly by, the twisting upward of the exits, the uncoiling of the access road.

"When I was younger, Milton, life seemed much more confusing to me. I had not learned yet to see through, only to see. Slowly I discovered how few things were opaque. Sometimes now I am overcome by the sadness of inconsequential details—the tattered lining of an old jacket, a leaf going to brown. A certain firmness has departed the earth, but it's the price a person pays for clarity."

"The price can be high," I say.

"There are sacrifices, terrible sacrifices. But I refuse to submit

to another man's insoluble problems. The times are extraordinary. Only the boldest solutions have any force." Correzano
reaches over and pats Ms. Daltrey on the knee. "Still, there are
moments when I don't think I could keep going if it weren't for
my friends."

Ms. Daltrey turns to me. "He's a lovely man, don't you
think?"

Suddenly, the car lurches to a stop. Correzano begins pounding
on the steering column. "There! There!"

I look up, follow the line traced by his pointing hand. Over our
heads is a large blue sign in three parts—a woman's head, breasts,
pubis, all resting on what I notice for the first time now is not
snow but pellets, small styrofoam pellets. Across the top is written the wondrous word: BEAUTY.

"Wha—?"

Ms. Daltrey sinks down into her seat, gazes open-mouthed out
the window. "Yes, yes, I see it. So much comes clear now."

Correzano lifts the valise from the floor, hands it back. "Make
sure the wire doesn't get kinked."

They both look at me, and I know I'll never understand my
stillness within this furious motion, how history lurches along its
unsteady way, but I realize a circle is perfection's shape and see
now, having gone round and round forever, how my own end has
come back to me. And I am lifting myself from the seat, climbing
out into flies, heat, milling ciphers all asweat, into cigarette
smoke and soft tar, crumbling curbstones, overflowing
dumpsters, ash, gas fumes, poison rain, into droves of commut-
ers maniacal with caffeine, into dank armpits and fungous toes
and double chins and soft gums and caries and splotchy hair,
through sewers and gutters and crowds of men wild to create, past
Dante's Florence and Diotima singing and Pythagorean holy men
in fields of sacred beans, past this nightmare of crushed feet,
mutilated labia, triangles, curves, corsets, stays, this rage for
something round and whole and living in the eye, and I feel love's
blight grow big inside of me, feel the mangled need that drives
men into flesh and out again, and I'm moving through the hiss of
paint sprayers, the smell of polyethylene, past trolleys piled with

knees, breasts, lashes, eyes, within a cavernous room where a woman hides her decomposing cheeks in a fold of barber's cloth and a beautician with a dueling scar flexes his triceps at me and a manicurist smacks her gum inside a wilderness of red hair and where from down a dark corridor Gloria appears, her arms flung up in the air, her knees churning, as she comes racing toward me.

"No," I shout, waving frantically. "R-run, run away!"

But too late, she's into my arms, her legs wrapped about my waist, her face against my neck, flesh on my flesh, and I stammer, "Mommy, find Mommy," beginning to tremble as I struggle to cling to the valise, my body going weak, "I'm not your father any—" and stop. For I've begun to sniff a strange scent, the heady sweetness of modeler's glue, and feel the hot breath in my ear, a rubbery pulsation in the clinch of her small thighs, and as Gloria's mouth begins to cover my mouth, her warm tongue to press against my teeth, I claw at her soft face, wrestle her arms from my head, shove her body away, no longer knowing myself, this life, any world that could have ever been mine. "Gloria?!"

"A surprise, Mr. Milton, something completely new." Bobby materializes from behind a stainless-steel injection mold, his face split in a broad grin. "Who knows how all of this started, where it will end? Return is impossible. Newness is all." He leers at me. "At last, you have everything your heart desires."

"But I don't want what my heart desires. I want...my family. Where's Agnes?"

And then I hear the unfamiliar laughter, look down into Gloria's smiling face, her wild blue eyes.

"Milton, darling," she says, laying her hand on my arm, "it's time to take your lovely young wife home."

And as I feel the charge shoot through the wires, as I hear it pass with an imperceptible click into the cap Ms. Daltrey has prepared perfectly, perfectly, just before the wave of flame lifts me heaven-ward, drives the stranger in my arms out through my spine and into the only pure moment human life ever knows, while this small fruit of horror and desire still presses herself against my heart as if to merge there with the deceitful craving that has destroyed the male mind, I know that the terror being born in my valise is the forgotten paradox of a beneficent nature fallen from a tree, the name of a computer company, love no longer innocent, and crushing my beloved to my chest, I remember sin. And we are airborne, and we are free, and my daughter and wife and future and flesh are one in the broiling hell of the infinitely possible in the sky.

Hmmm . . . 'twill not do, 'twill not do. Count them. Ah, they limp and jostle like a vanquished army. "Infinitely possible?" "Broiling?" As flaccid as a bellows! Insufficient for such knowing calculation seems, for this dark light, though "Enter not here ye who know nothing of geometry" and Socrates himself did call virtue computation, so conscience would be the font of numbers, but they do not come, they do not come. Is naught melodious and apt? Wandering, slow. But Paget says, freed now from sight's folly, affection doth spring forth of the spirit and this full holy, and there's a sweetness in youth's voice, I'd own as much, though yester ev'n of the Night as the city was as still as dark and I did lean upon this garden wall, an old odor rose up from the Earth and, strange longing, I did kneel and plunge this hand into the rimy ground as if to seek an answering grip there, and once again did know what it is to be bodily, to be fallen and mortally ripe, and was all the Night's night in a torment and could not becloud my always seeing Eye and wrestled with her, my incubus, as with Jehovah's messenger at Peniel, and she'd not be conquered, though I'm solitary enough for all that. Beware dotage. Why born of spirit and a virgin? Why not sprung full-pricked from the Almighty head? Why born of woman at all? Second mother, unblemished sister of infirm Eve, namesake of my enemy, mocker of too-weak eyes. I would be milked! And will be, Paget says, my utter sucked of this degenerate necessity, once again become like a starving man who, well-fed, doth forget hunger's pang. Heat, brain, bestir this silence, bring tumultuous sunrise of music and number, salt's smart, flaming cheeks, air fetid and sweet. A fart. You'll not ape Maeonides lowing like a sow. To know the Light but no flame, the dark without chill. A sacrament, they call it. There was little of that, little of that. What peace but among friends? What sacrament but conversation? Tell Paget, come, make merry talk, step with me into this garden, but speak no more of women. There's been too much said of women. Though Kathy, there was Kathy, and was she not one? And good? And gone. Ah, Kathy, had you been as stout as brave, what brawling sons we'd have made, and played long of the night on the organ, and walked through this garden, hand in hand, our steps wandering, yes, slow . . . taking our solitary . . . Hmmm . . .

METEMPSYCHOSIS

Dougherty dreams of second chances. He doesn't feel cheated so much as simply baffled by irreversability. Things happen. They don't happen again. He gazes across the room at the disemboweled Telecaster with its pots dangling, a pile of loose music sheets, four string packs, a peg winder, two tarnished tuning machines, and, here in front of him, Ponce's Fourth Prelude rippling thumb-frayed and yellow in a waft of greasy air blown in from the street. He has practiced his scales for three hours. If the phone does not ring, if a letter does not arrive, if no one comes to save his life, he will play this prelude, Sor's Etudes Eleven, Nineteen, and Twenty-one, Carulli's Capriccio, de Falla's *Hommage*, the Valse-Choro of Villa-Lobos, and miss all afternoon the same C sharp in measure two-seventy-seven of the Chaconne. He will forget to eat lunch. Even the cramps that begin just before dusk will not slow him, and the sibilance of his calloused fingertips will continue along the taut bronze coils until some arpeggio of semihemidemiquavers or a six-fret stretch wads up the muscles of his left hand into a mangled, fisty knot.

Dougherty nudges his wobbly footrest up against the still wobblier tripod of the music stand and wonders why, in a world where so much moves backward, a person must always move straight. He flops his hot palm over the cool rosewood shoulder of his guitar, lets his fingers dangle as loosely as jute.

He knows evening will find him, fork in hand, in a vinyl cafe chasing two forlorn enchiladas around a styrofoam plate or, later, seated beneath settling clouds of dessicated ocher stuffing in his magenta armchair paring his nails as darkness comes on. He does

45

not know if this is a life, does not know any longer how you would
determine such a thing. He allows himself to topple onto his
mattress shortly after midnight but neglects to remove his trousers and shirt. He has forgotten what sleep was like. Some time
before morning he will rise quietly, glide over to the window,
and, resting a hand on the spavined chiffonier, will gaze into the
night as if at something he hears there.

But not today—because today the phone is ringing. Dougherty's head comes up and with it the butt of the guitar which he
rights with his left knee dislodging the footrest that sends the
music stand plummeting toward the spruce rosette Doughtery
shields with his shoulder while stretching his arm through the
flapping wings of Ponce's airborne Prelude to pluck the brrrrrring-
ing receiver and crunch it to his ear.

"Dougherty here."

"On God's brown earth your only friend, but sidewalks, tram-
polines, astro-turf get better treated."

Esteban. "You're paid, finished, over, done, stopped, closed,
canceled, ended—"

"... book here within arm's length, got three hundred maybe
three-fifty names, phones—all union, all ready to come I say
come, to play I say play. Not a prima donna in the bunch. Players,
music boxes: put in your nickel, pop the lid, out comes your
sound. Simple. But Esteban—is he crazy? is he a marshmallow? is
he a saint?—Esteban calls you."

"Three hours studio time, eight masters, plus engineer's fee. I
have canceled checks—"

"Gotta white jigaboo singer in here from Boston this p.m.
None of your Fernando Sor-ass or goddamn Giuli-anal, but MCA
subsidiary has her on a one-record contract and wants to boot her.
It'll melt in a warehouse but they're paying union scale if you
want it."

Somewhere in Dougherty's chest just beneath his broken heart
something twisted, small, and very ugly says, "Yeah. I want it."

"Bring your Telecaster, put on a satin shirt, and swagger like
an R&B man. We'll run you through the console with the synthesizer."

"Time?"

"Two-thirty." He's gone.

And Dougherty is jockeying the flattened black vinyl alligator onto a crosstown bus thinking that in a sense now it is already too late, that the cadence would have to be deceptive, a falling backward to the sixth or at least a refusal to go on—the major seventh with its topple toward tonic suddenly arrested, hanging there. He thinks of the Villa-Lobos Fifth Estudios with its denial of music's gravitation, not simply as postponement anymore, but as probability's suspension—section V of Britten's *Nocturnal*, the stringing together of unresolvable fourths, poised, prepared, tensed, eternally waiting to fall, to fall, to fall. He shudders. Sound has always had this tangibility for Dougherty: Bach's dark rhombi, Duarte's delicate planes. Bream began guitar at age twelve, even Parkening was eleven; Paganini's health was gone, Weiss' thumb nearly bitten off, and the eighteen-year-old Django with half a left hand burned away. Dougherty glances at his own long fingers, smiles, pats smugly at the silk wings of his white tie, gazes out the window, smooths his crisp shirt front in the large mirror just behind the stage curtain. He ignores the fatuous house manager wadding his coattails and glancing at his watch. The program will begin with the Chaconne, a bold declaration, and so, while lowering the bass string, Dougherty has cheated slightly on equal temperament to guarantee himself at least one perfect fifth. The lights are up. Guitar in hand Dougherty glides through the curtain, chin high, does not acknowledge the audience. There is a shocked silence—the auditorium is jammed, tiers upon tiers; Dougherty feels their eyes—then from everywhere an explosion of cheers, banging of seats, wild applause as Dougherty swings from the bell pull, lurches into the aisle, stumbles over a pair of swollen calves in heavy brown shoes, dodges the lethal hook of a newspaper-reader's umbrella, garbles a hot-faced apology to a young woman's breast he has somehow managed to pinch, and pulls his case from the clinch of the hissing doors as the bus lumbers away.

In the studio the foyer and control room are empty, the console off. Dougherty steps behind the board and gazes through the

engineer's window at a tall thirtyish white woman in gabardine
suit and tan pumps playing what sounds like from the corridor—
Dougherty lifts a headset to one ear, plugs the jack, flips the
preamp toggles—what actually is a weird keyboard setting of
Bach's B Minor Mass with some fancy Baroque extemporization
in the continuo.

"Where's the band?" he asks as Esteban swings around the
corner in a yellow body shirt with half a tiparillo sticking out of
his face.

"Miss Lily White brought her own rhythm masters. We fill,
dub, mix, go home."

"You said union."

"MCA calls, tells me it's contract, naturally I assume..." He
shrugs, waves Dougherty out of the control room. "Name's Lilac
or Lola or something."

And Dougherty would like to believe he's outraged but has
been poor long enough to know better. So he finds himself in the
corridor, the belly of the alligator slapping his thigh as he wonders
if her left-hand part is not a little too rich, too active, without
enough sustain, almost as if she's been listening to a stride player,
something he won't remember to ask her about until later that
night in bed (bed?!), after he's plugged once more into the over-
taxed Fender Princeton, praying as always it won't blow them all
to hell, hung the headset on his neck, snapped trills until
Estaban's set levels, all the while watching as she doubles the
octaves at A, her thumb and pinky stretching like gull wings, and
him thinking how strange it is that a single note can reappear in
two positions, a doubling of hertz like space or time, 220 and 440,
one note but somehow two. He thinks her unsung kyrie should
not be here, thinks she should not be here, he should not be here,
thinks maybe if he closes his eyes and just listens they won't be,
but knows that an hour of this dross will feed him for a week and
so cranks up his potentiometer and lets rumble the raunchiest
shuffle his weary indice, medio, and anular can muster. He
lowers his eyes, tries not to notice that the piano has stopped, that
Esteban is yammering through the phones, that the toes of the tan
pumps seem planted upon the carpet directly beneath his head.

"Hi, I'm Lilah."

Dougherty's fingers droop on the fretboard. His eyes creep cautiously up the pumps, legs, skirt, jacket. Her black hair is as kinky as a Tijuana brothel. She wears her eyeglasses low on her nose. Her lips are very dark.

"You're Dougherty," she grins. "They told me about you."

And so Dougherty will not play the Chaconne this evening, is perfect for one hour as the tapes roll and re-roll, then for half an hour more after the chorus arrives, makes supper of an egg dish with a fancy name, has too many gimlets, sours, tonics, deposits his entire day's wages into the accumulated palms of the waiters and taxidrivers in three corners of the city, and will find himself sometime after two a.m. sitting on the edge of a bed on top of a wadded-up brassiere in a poorly lit hotel room struggling stupidly with a knot in his wingtips as two bare arms entangle about his chest and pull him backward into the depths of quilt and down.

"... learn to play continuo like a stride player as a blues singer in Boston?" Dougherty's asking.

"Had a gospel choir in D.C. once. Fifty black Baptists. You got any dope?"

"Drugs?" Dougherty's shoe gives suddenly, sails upward, and strikes the floor with a frightful thud.

"You're funny, y'know that? They didn't tell me you'd be funny."

A large mouth covers the lower half of Dougherty's face. "Mmmff, mmmff! 'They'?"

"Here, let's get those pants."

Dougherty claws at his fly as he feels himself being dragged from the bed. In the shadows he glimpses a large plum-colored nipple, a row of bright teeth, black ringlets tumbling over one eye. "Hey! Let me unfasten them first!"

"Hurry, hurry."

The clip on his waistband pops, the fabric hisses over his knees. "Wh-what is this?"

Lilah leaps onto his chest. "Love," she says.

Dougherty dreams of a place where the world cannot go. In the darkness in the hole in the rosewood box: he has always wanted to live inside a circle. He'd like to seep into his hands, dribble out his callouses, purl down the fretboard and plash into the rivers of twisted grain. He wakes up alone in a hotel bed this morning, his head in convulsions and half his practice day gone. When he gets home he finds in his mailbox a ragstock envelope requesting forty-seven cents additional postage to return his audition tapes and three announcements of master classes conducted by unknowns at extortionists' fees. He plays the *Mazurka Appasionata* of Barrios, Ponce's Valse, Turina's Fandanguillo and Rafaga, the Gavotte, Bouree, and Gigue from Bach's Lute Suite Number Four, Sor's Minuets in C and D, Milan's six Pavanas, Weiss' *Tombeau sur la morte de M. Comte de Logy*, Rodrigo's Sarabanda and stops for the phone four times: the same wrong number twice, once for a sweaty voice that would like to sell him a new roof for his fine old downtown home one of which, incidentally, if he doesn't own would he like to buy, and the final time for a nervous, soft-spoken youth who, well, just wants to know if his thighs are hairy. When the horn shorts-out on the abandoned Dodge beneath his window, Dougherty is about to miss again the C sharp in measure two-seventy-seven of the Chaconne but instead props his guitar on its stand, upending his coffee cup on an unread issue of *Gitarre & Laute*, and takes the train to a sanitary room in a remote suburb where he sits in the dark and watches Anaheim die. There hasn't been any light here for more months than Dougherty can remember, but in the slatted glow from the window he can tell Anaheim's eyes are shaded and that his skin is the color of Spanish onions, that mortality is gathering force within him, seeking this darkness just outside the thin, thin sheath of flesh.

"Did I tell you Farlow once tried to buy the Rubio Bream gave me? Kept saying he could put a pickup on it. I said, man, that spruce isn't a thirty-second of an inch thick. What you want to put a magnet on it for? He just grinned. God, was he ever a homely bastard."

Sometimes Dougherty wraps a sweetroll in saran and carries it with him to this room because he knows Anaheim enjoys watching him eat. The train costs eighty cents each way and Dougherty keeps the stubs as a way of marking time. Paper metronome. He'd like to ask Anaheim about time, about canons and perpetuum mobile, about how in the Scherzo of Schubert's opus 100 the parts can repeat each other exactly one bar behind, why the circle of fifths returns to its beginning, why there are refrains, encores, reprises, and why Dougherty's time is running out. If you make a mistake in the middle of a performance, continue as if nothing has occurred. Anaheim squirms beneath the tubes and blankets, twists toward Dougherty like a beached seal.

"You still fucking up the Chaconne?"

Dougherty smiles.

"I took Montgomery once to hear Segovia at the Smithsonian. Afterwards he kept calling it the chuck-cone." Anaheim laughs, gazes out at Dougherty from beneath his visor. "Your problem's the fingering. You'll never get it with Segovia's fingering."

They talk about the pigeons the city tries to keep off the statue in the traffic circle outside the room where Anaheim first showed Dougherty a flatted fifth chord, about how Carl Sandburg liked to have his picture taken with Llobet's guitar until a student of Papadopoulos asked him to play it once, or about the time Bream got looped and claimed to Anaheim and Byrd he'd been a jazz man and so with Byrd faking bass and Anaheim on rhythm he started laying down these riffs right out of Giuliani.

"Making any money?" Anaheim asks.

"Studio work. Throw-aways mostly."

"Agent call about your demos?"

Dougherty shakes his head.

They are silent.

"Back when Farlow and me were playing, we didn't have jazz musicians or rock musicians or classical musicians. You played guitar, you played it all. Like you." Anaheim's spine scratches away at the pillow. "Sixties ruined all that."

But Dougherty is already standing, gathering his ticket, the copy of *Guitar Player* he'll read on the train, the wad of saran, thinking that playing it all may simply mean playing nothing one day and wondering how long until the morning he sits down before the loose folios of Villa-Lobos, Castelnuovo-Tedesco,

Tarrega, Martin, Ferrer, places the Ramirez over his knee, raises his hand like a parasol, and hears his brain scream, NO! How long before he is Anaheim wired for death in a sanitary box, vanished from Earth but for the occasional dotted sixteenth hop in the solo of a few hundred teenagers and a second-rate professional or two who on any given night after a fourth scotch will lean back against the bar and say, "Had this teacher, weird cat, used to play with the old-timers—Burrell, Kessel, Ellis—druggy, I think, but man could he ever play bop." Dougherty half-turns at the doorjamb, his hand on the knob, and glances back into the darkness he thinks is maybe his heart.

"Don't bar for the A." Anaheim holds up his left hand, tubes dangling, wags his index finger stiffly back and forth against a fretboard of air.

"Huh?"

"That's Segovia's trick, keeps everyone else from playing it, the Chaconne. If you got fingers like a chimpanzee, then maybe you can reach the accidentals, but you and me..."

Anaheim's face is dark beneath the sunshade but Dougherty thinks he's smiling.

"Don't bar until you absolutely have to."

And so Dougherty is out the door and onto the train and past the Dodge with its horn still blaring and up the stairwell and into his apartment again, or nearly, climbing the last steps within sight of the door thinking there's something squalid about the violence you work upon yourself, the suspicious odor of self-mutilation, and yet recalling what Brouwer said once—or was it Barbosa-Lima—that if Weiss' compositions resulted from a half-severed hand, then the injury was a small price: noble sentiments, Dougherty thinks, for men with ten fingers. Still, everyone loses his hands; only a few know what it is to have had them. Which reminds him of the night in the Muncipal Theatre when Basset-faced Segovia with his thumbs like putty knives first showed Dougherty and five thousand others what it is to have had them, a night that left Dougherty repeating for the next twenty-three years the whisp-whisps of Segovia's fingers on the too-fast arpeggios of Villa-Lobos' Second Prelude or the caress of his medio's pulpy underbelly on the false harmonics of the *Nocturnal's* variation VI, a night that boxed him up in silence too dense to ever unpackage and left him longing to be all hand, perfect hand, that sent him with his Fender Jaguar the next morning to Rhythm City where the pock-cheeked guy with the limp and baggy eyes—all the players called him "Fritz" but Dougherty saw him open his checkbook once and it said "Rudy"—told him the strings Segovia used weren't gut but nylon ever since Albert Augustine persuaded Olga Coelho to trade in her kitty bowels back in January of forty-four and that, yes, maybe they could make a deal, thirty-five dollars and his old guitar for the Japanese model over there with a soft-shell case which, of course, Dougherty took knowing he'd been taken, but not caring because, while Fritz/ Rudy climbed the ladder to pull down the carton, Dougherty managed to slip the copy of Bach transcriptions out of the display case into his shirt hoping it would be the right one which later he found out, yes, it was. Dougherty smiles. From Johnny B. Goode to the Chaconne in twenty-four hours, a thought so delightful now it makes Dougherty leap the last three steps, grab the bannister, swing up onto the landing, and impale his right nostril on the outstretched finger of Mrs. Stampf.

"Mr. Dougherty, I'd be careful of the Jews!"

Dougherty smiles, nods, retrieves his nose.

"There was Jews on the fire escape all night long. You could hear the clanging of they's boots."

"Natashe! Natashe! Tell the boy to bring here his pistol."

Dougherty hears the click-click and hum of Mrs. Stampf's electric sister rolling down the corridor. Mrs. Stampf places her face between Dougherty's nose and his door.

"Jews as big as trees, Mr. Dougherty."

"Bring here his pistol we can shoot'em!" Click-click-click, hmmmmmmmmmmm.

Dougherty excuses himself, feints left, lunges right, jabs his key at the lock. Won't go. Inside the apartment his phone has started ringing.

"It's they's gold heels that's clanging..."

"Boom, boom, boom, shoot 'em. Hee, heeeeeee!"

The key goes, the door gives, Dougherty falls on his face. But manages to kick the door closed again before Mrs. Stampf's sister runs him over — hmmmmmmmmmmmmmmmmmmmmmmmmm, click-click, WHUMP! Dougherty pulls the phone off the mandolin case he uses for a coffee table beside the magenta chair and crushes the receiver to his ear.

"You need me?" her voice asks from very far away, a question like no other, the tonic toward which Dougherty's cadence this whole day has been plunging. Dougherty stares at the spreading blob of rust in the carpet beneath the window beside the door.

"Yes."

And before he can replace the receiver in the cradle she's across town in a bus and two cabs up the four flights of stairs through his door out of her dress into his bed and has her arms wound twice around his chest so tight he doesn't even have time to breathe much less ask himself what the hell he thinks he's doing, or if not that fast then fast just the same, before he can realize what you and I've already figured out: that, Dougherty, poor slob, you'll be lucky to get out of this story alive.

"Oh, I don't know really," she is saying when he wakes, her cheek propped on one palm, the sheet billowing whitely beneath her left breast which has oozed itself tear-shaped and slightly flattened onto the mattress. "Just somebody I knew once. I used to get around a lot, got two degrees I never used, then went back to night-school, studied Greek then opera. Somehow I ended up with this contract, so I said, y'know, it's something to do."

Dougherty wants to push the loose hair away from her eyes but hesitates. "So after the record . . . ?"

"Record?"

"That MCA's going to press."

She throws back her head, howls, "Garbage, garb-AGE!" then shrugs her shoulders so that her breast stretches out then squashes oval again. "I used to have a telephone answering service. That was in Detroit. Let me sleep late. Then I drove a taxi, in Chicago, but I got stuck up—"

"Stuck up?"

"They were kids. Nice kids. Nervous and really polite. I gave 'em all I had." She smiles, "But it made me sad, so I got a job teaching high school. Band and chorus. But I fell in love with my students—seventeen-year-olds—and that scared me so I got out." She turns over on her back. "I've never wanted to be good at anything."

When Dougherty wakes again the sun is coming through the window and she's still lying like that, her arms raised—a little like wings—her hands behind her head. He looks at her a long time, believing she's asleep, but then she says:

"You're in trouble, aren't you?"

Dougherty dreams of a number, one and one more, that would make one One again. Of a hole as clean and empty as his mailbox all day long. He eats this dream for breakfast and digests it by nine. He buttons it, zips it, sweats it all morning in the noxious air from the street, coughs it into a handkerchief he never remembers to wash. He jerks it off, pisses it away, drinks it from a dirty glass he finds in his cabinet, and before five-thirty has begun to hear it even in the sounds of sirens and dogfights and motorcycles. His enchilada this evening looks so dejected he can't bring himself to cut it, can't even watch it very long without wondering whether there was ever any real magic in Segovia's hands or if the sound he heard then was merely the sound he hears at night standing before the chiffonier gazing into the mirror as the stars twist by, if in fact this whole zany mix of events is not more orderly than he'd like to believe, a moronic, petty fate: "n" hundred musicians wanting to perform for "n-ty" audiences, or for merely "n", or even 1/"nth"—not really a matter of persistence, attrition, luck at all.

Dougherty slides out of the vinyl booth, drops his tray, fork, uneaten enchilada in the trash can, THANK YOU, and starts down the walk listening to his own silence thinking how much nicer it is than sound. Outside vans and semis snort through the dark. His mistakes seem so simple to him now, only he can't understand how he could have not made them. 110, 220, 440, 880—return of the same in a new position: one note but somehow two. A second chance? Or merely noise. He lies in bed trying very

hard to be nothing, to let sleep pass over him like nausea, to
ignore the ringing of the phone.

But later the banging on his door can't be ignored.

"Arithmetic," Esteban announces, pushing past groggy
Dougherty, striding into the room and perching like an omnivorous canary on the arm of the magenta chair. "Hours, dollars, feet
of tape, six players, seventy bucks a date, sixteen tracks, A at 440,
dominant seven if you want blues."

Dougherty shakes sense into his brain and girns at the clock on
his refrigerator. "Good Christ, it's four a.m.!"

Esteban shoves a finger at Dougherty's chest. "Numbers,
prima donna. That's music, that's business, that's facts and the
hardest, coldest is: your number's not up because it's too high."

"Maybe if you wrote it all down on a check for me..."

"Thirty-seven Dougherty, thirty-seven. That's eleven years
too many."

"Asshole."

"Get mad if you want but you're arguing with the calculator."
Esteban leans closer. "I'm worried about you, kid. You're killing
yourself. Laid out that dough in my studio, played till you bled,
haven't got a nibble."

"I haven't heard from all the agencies yet."

"Haven't got a nibble. You're good, prima donna. You got
hands other sidemen would kill for, read charts like pictures, stay
cool. Nothing you can't play two tries. I could keep you afloat.
Ten, twelve dates a week..."

"Sidemen die unhappy."

"It'd keep you in cornbread. And Esteban's got some highbrow
connections, too. Feruzzi, Anders, Barrueco. I even got a call
from Bobri once."

"What is it you want, Esteban?"

"Get that bitch out of my studio!"

"Huh?"

"Re-mix this, call back in the vocal group, add a sax here..."

"How should I—"

"I got a gig and two dates this Thursday says you can find a
way. Otherwise eat nylon!" The door slams behind him.

"Where'd you spend the night, Dodo?" Lilah's asking him. "Or did your phone go on strike?"

Dougherty feels the heat from his palm through the receiver, watches the worm of sweat wiggle down his arm. He tries to believe he was once vigorous enough to be deceitful, that candor in him is anything but lack of character, but only wants right now to play so hard, loud, and fast that his life will shrink up smaller than his hands. He remembers selling his Dobro, dreadnaught, and last Telecaster to buy his Ramirez, remembers having to buy the Telecaster back again.

"I wondered, maybe today..." He doesn't believe he's doing this. "After you finish at the stu —"

"I phoned New York yesterday."

"Maybe you could even leave early, huh? Esteban says —"

"Talked to my friend at MCA. He gave me this number of —"

"An early drink, supper. Around three. We could even take the whole afternoon —"

"Dougherty, shut up."

There's no air in Dougherty's head. He gazes out the window, thinks, yes, I will now cave in.

"You know Shaw Concerts?"

"Uh...handle Lorimer?"

"Williams, Barbosa-Lima." She giggles. "You'd better be as good as they say you are cause Doris, Dolores, Dora...something, junior agent there, she wants to hear your tapes."

They? They? They? They? They? They? They? They? They? They? And Dougherty is moving again, briefcase under his arm, long legs cramped behind the corrugated back of the next seat as the bus farts its way from stop light to stop light, throwing him left, right, forward, back, trying to shake him from this dream that something is happening at last. The thought that diligence counts for nothing at all, this suspicion has his colon twisted up like a spit curl, has him terrified, and yet if something actually *is* happening hasn't he always suspected that behind Dowland's irregular phrasing is no pattern, no inevitability, that nothing brings you back to the beginning but the composer's arbitrary decision that, hmmmm, perhaps now it's time. Time for what?

Somewhere there is laughter but Dougherty can't hear it. He stands, tramples the legs of his seatmate, pulls the bell cord loose from its rings, grabs someone's newspaper for balance, puts his hand through a young man's hat, trips on his own shoelace, just as the lurch of the bus bounces him down the steps, out the doors, and onto the sidewalk in a crumpled heap. All his life he's wanted to be whole. He pays three dollars to post his tapes special delivery, insured, return receipt requested, gets a taxi to the studio, refuses to look at Esteban who is screaming something salacious, and before night, after a dinner of edible food prepared in his own kitchen by the walking, irrefutable argument that God exists and wants to do Dougherty a favor, finds himself drowning in mouths, tongues, flesh, hair, a death more peaceful than sleep.

He wakes sitting in the straight-backed chair in the sanitary room beside Anaheim's bed.

"Broads? Look-a-me! Three old ladies and a twenty-two-year-old I put through Georgetown and I rot here alone. Talk about broads after you've signed the contract."

"She wants to help."

"Yeah, like Carmen wanted to help. I warm up Woody Allen a week at Hurt's place, two weeks in the Village, then Allen sends me packing with bus fare. I get home licking sores and walk in on Carmen's orgy. Got lonely, she says." Anaheim rolls back and forth underneath the sheet, lifts his hands as if to push off a ledge, then lets them fall onto his thighs. "We'd been married eight months."

Dougherty stares at a scab on Anaheim's wrist as big as a penny. He wants to peel off the sunvisor, dive into Anaheim's face and drag him back to the surface of his skin. He'd like to hear Anaheim play "Stardust" again, the old way, chiming with his fingernail like Farlow used to do, or "Take Five" with the dotted thirty-second no one else ever hit clean, or the Van Heusen tunes, or "Sermonette," or "El Manha de Carnivale," or . . .

"She got you practicing harder? Making money? Stopped you barring for the A?"

"The whole turn-around works off the A."

Anaheim snorts. "You think that means you gotta make the chord?"

"It's easier."

"Yeah? Wait till you have to change positions." Anaheim leans closer, his eyes suddenly wet, whispers, "You bar cause you're scared, kid, cause you want to hold to something. Let go, okay? Let go."

Let go of what? he wonders hugging her so tight her chin snuggles into the cup between his clavicle and shoulder and her shoulder fits up under his arm and her belly feels as smooth and round as, oh hell! there's nothing as smooth and round as her belly right now. Let go of the contract he doesn't have? Of a phone call that's got to come soon if Dora/Dolores/Doris is really interested? Of this life where everything that was going to happen maybe already has? Let go of... the Ramirez tumbles from his knee, cracks the footrest, and, with the hundred twenty-five pounds of pressure from the nylon strings, snaps the head loose and sends it flying back at the Telecaster that tumbles from his knee, cracks the amplifier, and, with the sixty-five pounds of pressure from the super slinky strings, snaps the head loose and sends it flying back at the Gurian dreadnaught that tumbles from his knee, cracks the guitar case, and, with the three hundred eighty pounds of pressure from the bronze strings, snaps the head off and sends it flying back at the last chance Dougherty has that anything could ever happen good to him at all.

"Tomorrow, Dodo, we go shopping."

"Shopping?"

"I knew you'd be threadbare, but no one ever told me you'd look like a bum."

"No one who?"

"And we'll put some flesh on you, buy some groceries. How long since you deviled an egg?"

"I'm not sure I like eggs."

"If we wait till you're sure, you'll starve."

Dougherty changes positions. "How long... before you finish at the studio?"

A week passes before she replies. "Why?"

"Because they're kicking you out the union, prima donna." Esteban's voice is as cool as the switchblade that slits your throat. "I got a bill collector coming over your place tonight with an invoice for seven hundred dollars—tapes, reels, engineer's fees. This afternoon Papadopoulos calls up the American Classical Guitary Society to let'em know your name's death. You're through, Dougherty."

"Why me, Esteban?"

"She's costing more money than I can count. MCA just reads me the contract everytime I call. I hear you think you've got an in at Shaw?"

Dougherty squeezes the receiver. "Shaw how shaw who shaw wha—"

"Doris Goldman was her name. Pal of Feruzzi. He owed me a favor."

"Look, it isn't my fault you signed a sucker contract."

"Don't argue, prima donna. Pay, act, move, do. The numbers are on my side. You think she can manage your act, wipe your nose, buy you a concert hall, make you twenty-three again?"

"Go to hell."

"Bill collector's six-six and black as your name!"

And Dougherty no longer knows where she comes from or how she appears. Does not know if she lives here in this room or if the sudden absence of stains and strewn pages, the awful silence in the afternoons, if the warmth beside his skin and the musky taste of dark hair, if these are parts of his own life now or are merely things that come, linger, disappear. He eats real food, plays for an hour, maybe two, forgets his mail, grows restless until she returns. He has begun to taste and smell things. When the phone rings, he answers: "Hurry! Hurry home!" He's dying into someone else's life and each morning feels his fingers growing stiffer on strings he no longer hears.

"Why?" she asks again, still waiting.

"Esteban called. Says he's done in Shaw Concerts."

She laughs. "He's gonna have a truck hit me next week, settle for my life insurance. What a sweet ass he's getting to be. You disappointed?''

Dougherty thinks the answer to this question should be as obvious as nuclear fission, but it's not, even to him. "I suppose." Suppose?!

"Guy I used to know in Philly—"

"Didn't you ever use to know any *women*?"

" —worked for the arts-in-the-schools thing. He might could set up a high school tour for you. Not very glorious, but you get paid real money to play whatever you like. Taste this bleu I got downtown.''

Dougherty takes the cheese from the knife, feels his nostrils widen. "You know, sometimes I'm not sure there's anything I really like to play."

"Producer friend of mine in L.A. once—"

"L.A.?"

"I sold real estate there then ran a laundromat. He told me you could tell a sideman from a soloist because the sideman doesn't really like music. He just likes to play. Duane Allman, for instance. He was a good sideman."

"And the soloist?"

She smiles, looks into Dougherty's eyes for a month or two. "You, Dodo, are a soloist."

And the next morning she's gone. Doughtery upends the apartment, finds the phone number of a Renaissance consort that wants him for lute parts, a Juicy Fruit wrapper, the missing folio from Ponce's Preludes, an ivory bridge pin, four string packs, a peg winder, two tarnished tuning machines, but not a piece of her. He dashes down the stairwell where Mrs. Stampf is denouncing the butchery of about a million Catholic infants, grabs a taxi and terrorizes the prissy desk clerk at the hotel, but all Dougherty gets is a Boston phone where, when he calls it, nobody speaks English and an address scribbled out longhand that appears to be #%$*!+¢, Kudzu, Puerto Rico, ᒧᒧᒧᒧᒧ. She paid cash; nobody saw her leave. At the studio a gospel quartet in powder blue jump suits with satin epaulets and more zippers than Dougherty can count is hitting an A minor sixth chord in the foyer. When Dougherty asks for Esteban the tenor slides contemptuously up to the dominant seventh and rolls his eyes toward the console.

Esteban doesn't know him.

"All I want's her phone number."

"Busy this morning, pal. Come back Sunday."

"Your headache's over. She's gone. Just give me the guy's name at MC—"

"You want studio time, see the appointment secretary."

"There is no appointment secre—"

"See the receptionist."

"There is no recep—"

When Dougherty gets home Mrs. Stampf's electric sister has somehow gotten a pistol and is shooting pedestrians from the fire escape outside Dougherty's window. Dougherty slips past the police cordon, down the service alley, through the broken window in the unlocked janitor's pantry, up the stairwell, and onto the landing as Mrs. Stampf comes dashing down the corridor waving a kitchen knife shrieking something about circumcision and eyeing Dougherty's fly. The damn key still won't go, then does, the door gives, Dougherty falls on his face but manages to kick the door closed on Mrs. Stampf's hand. "Yeeeeeeeeow!" Hmmmm-mmmmmmmm, click-click, "Heee, heee!" BLAM, BLAM, BLAM. And three bullet holes appear in Dougherty's door. Dougherty barricades the doorway and retreats to the magenta armchair where he sits for thirteen hours believing if he stares at his phone long enough, hard enough, it will ring. Which it finally does a little after three a.m., waking him with a lurch that nearly tears the cord from the wall.

"Can't . . . hardly . . . breathe, kid."

Anaheim.

"Goddamn half a lung . . . rotten liver."

"I'll be right—"

"Naw. It's . . . not time."

"Scared?" Dougherty asks.

"You got it."

They are silent.

"Listen. At my place...key behind the shutter beside the door.... Get my Rubio, the Johnny Smith, too, if you want.... Don't let those bitches—"

"Tomorrow?"

"Yeah. Go early." Anaheim wheezes. "Play'em, sell'em, I don't care."

"I can come now, to the hospital, if you..."

Anaheim pauses. "You're a good player, Dougherty. Just a little tight's all. She leave you?"

"She left."

"Everything does."

He's gone.

And Dougherty dreams the dream he no longer remembers. Of a time he hadn't become all he isn't and so could dream only what he is, a time when memory was for nothing at all. He hunts himself inside the armchair where the foam has gone to flake, peers through his sleep into the lampshade, and sifts the dust that spills from the molding when six hours later he slams the door, catches the westbound train, and zig-zags between transfer stops to a world of lawnmowers, skinned knees, carports, clogged drains. He knows a circle is perfection's shape and that we can be sure of this because once sometime, somewhere we each stood with one palm upon a dusty chiffonier and gazed up into the stars to hear perfection's sound, but he still tastes her hair in his mouth, feels her hip rubbing his hip, the stiff prod of her toes in the dark, and so wonders, standing here in this lilac and mauve living room Anaheim might have owned but, despite the Thunderbirds in the drive and the photos of Farlow, Bream, Joe Pass, Lester Polsfuss as a gawky kid, could never have come home to—and so wonders standing here now if one instrument could truly be the sum of all the extinct violas da mano, vihuelas, chitarriglias, quinternas, and lutes, if Luis Milan still lives in Segovia's hands, and if the sound Dougherty already dreads making this afternoon in his clammy apartment just before the cramps bend his thumb to his palm, if this sound will be even a whit richer for all Dougherty's destroyed producing it. Dougherty finds Anaheim's guitars in a bedroom with two portraits of a blonde teenager on one wall, a stripped bed, a chest dripping cords and pick-up wire from its drawers, manuscript paper spread out over everything. The Johnny Smith is still resting on the practice amp as if Anaheim had just laid it down there, but the low E is tarnished at the octave and so Dougherty figures it hasn't been moved in better than six months, maybe a year. The Rubio's in the closet, its bridge coming up at the butt. Dougherty runs water on a rag, stuffs it into the string box in the case beside the neckrest and with a guitar in each hand starts down the hall wondering how much of Anaheim died when he leaned the Johnny Smith up like that, straightened slowly from the cafe chair, and holding himself up with one hand on the doorjamb and an elbow on an opened chest drawer phoned Emergency realizing he'd never finish the arrangement he'd been struggling with all morning long—lots of Montgomery's octaves over a tonic/flat-five bass line with suspended fourth chords doing something weird just before the first upbeat of every other bar—realizing this progression would hang there, unresolved, incomplete, like a pole vaulter caught by a snapshot in midair, conclusive proof of gravity's weakness, that Anaheim's solo would never become itself, just as the sound Dougherty's heard standing beside his chiffonier each night has never become itself, just as Dougherty hasn't, just as nothing ever does.

And Dougherty stops right there. Through the open door he sees a spaniel disemboweling a trash bag, two tricycles, a blue Ford backing jerkily from the drive and hurrying away. For a long time he hasn't permitted himself these thoughts and now that he has, they fall with little clunks onto the heap of old notes and fears that are crammed into Dougherty's skull like beer cans in a dumpster. Something's begun whose end may be him. He plops the Rubio on the loveseat, takes the Johnny Smith from its case, and starts back down the hall already trying to hear the same line, the same progression, the same cadence Anaheim heard on the morning his body told him no, knowing this inevitability is what Dougherty's sought ever since Segovia drove the Chaconne and twenty-two years of sleepless nights into his adolescent brain, ever since Fritz/Rudy with his greasy smile took him for much more than money and ever since he first dared hope there was a good way to complete every convergence, not fate but something as lovely as one and won are too. Gravitas. And so with Anaheim's guitar on his knee, the stand top-heavy but standing, the jacks plugged, the pots on, and all the confidence annihilation brings, with the marvelous weight of a life badly lived pressing down upon his hands, and failure, failure, failure in his heart, he flips the toggles, cleans the worst of the grime from the strings, positions the music, and with the sirens growing louder by the second, with time as absent as the zero which is the egg of all things, Dougherty plays.

"Freeze!"

"RELAX!"

"Don't move!"

"Keep your hands where we can see 'em!"

Dougherty's out of his chair then knocked right back into it again and going over backwards, the Johnny Smith bounces off the floor, Dougherty catches himself on the bed. Five blue torsos with gold buttons and angry badges on the tits float in front of his nose. There seem to be these revolvers.

"Noooooobody wants trouble," one torso is saying. "Nooo-ooobody wants any trouble."

"...s-some mistake..."

"Anyone you know, Miss?"

Over his knee and through an armpit Dougherty sees the portrait of the blonde teenager grow eight years older and say, "...saw the front door open, so I drove to Miss Burnett's house, she's the lady—"

"I-I'm Dougherty."

"I said RELAX!"

Two nightsticks move in front of Dougherty's face like windshield wipers.

"...lady up the street. And she called you, I mean, the police. She called the police."

"Your father, Anaheim. I'm his—"

"Didn't I say RELAX!?''

"Noooooooooobody wants trouble.''

"These are very valuable instruments,'' the portrait is explaining to a pair of sunglasses.

Dougherty smiles at the nearest nightstick, speaks in a polite voice. "Her father, you see, he phoned, said come by, key behind the shutter, pick up—''

"Liar!''

"No, I'm your father's friend.''

But something's wrong because the portrait has whirled around, marched up to him, and is jabbing her finger into Dougherty's eye. Her mouth reads like an obituary, which makes Dougherty shudder, mistaking it for his own, before too late he understands.

"My father never called you.''

"He did. Last night. He told me—''

"Didn't!''

"I'd fallen asleep, beside the phone and—''

"Didn't call! Didn't call!''

"He must have mentioned my name. I'm—''

"My father's been dead over a week.''

And so Dougherty won't play for us after all, won't practice the Chaconne this evening, won't feel his thumb cramp, won't ever become anything more than he is despite the accumulated momentum of this rage, his restless nights, all the unplayed music he has somehow managed to hear. Or maybe because of these things. He slumps down into his chair and tries hard not to imagine what he'll be forced to say before this episode mercifully concludes, all the grim faces he'll have to forget, the sweaty rooms he'll pass through, for he's about to realize what he's been trying not to know for the length of this whole story, for twenty-two years now, for as long as you and I have been struggling to protect the last remnants of our own childhood, about to realize that standing beside the chiffonier staring up at the stars that make no music, that rising like this each night believing the sounds in his head were so massive they'd long since crushed his heart, that all this time he's never once heard repeated what Segovia played for fifteen-year-old him and five thousand others, what Bach wrote and Mendelssohn, Schumann, Willhelm, Hermann, Brahms, Raff, Busoni rearranged, what Anaheim had tried to teach him not to mangle beyond recognition, that the reason he never sharps the C every afternoon is because he never hears it sharp, because he doesn't want to hear it sharp, because what if he did and it was only music? about to confront this most perverse species of human folly, the plain fact that nothing makes him hornier than the possibility of his own death, and so will end up here with his left elbow hooked over the bed, his legs spread out over a scramble of sheet music and guitar cords, surrounded by strangers who want to hurt him, having been given the chance to love the world or be crushed by it and furiously, achingly, terrifyingly conscious now that he chose the latter because he found annihilation imaginable whereas love has become for him something infinitely strange. And he clutches his face in his hands, feels his eyes seep through his fingers, and Dougherty has begun to cry.

"He...he can't be dead."

"I've never seen this man before in my life. He's a criminal."

"Keep you hands out where we can see 'em!"

"RELAX!"

"He...he can't be dead."

"Noooooobody wants any trouble."

And I don't need to tell you the rest of this. Dougherty's been had. Me, you—we've dreamed his life so many times, and listen, if there's anything you don't know about it, consider yourself lucky. Things'll get worse, continue, get worse. At a certain point in a man's life, what's wrong is just wrong and all the realizations in the world won't change that. In the end after massive amounts of prolonged humiliation, injustice, failure, rejection, and suffering, Dougherty will lose his youth, his money, his health, his friends, and be forgotten, die alone. It's enough to make you never want to read another story as long as you live. But I admit it, bleakness like this is hard to endure, even for serious people like you and me, and so some mornings if I wake up early and can't get back to sleep, say around 5:30, 6:00, and the sky is the color of a Siamese cat's eyes, and the air is that dry cool of October, and I'm all alone, well, then I imagine another ending to Dougherty's story. Don't get me wrong, this isn't the *real* ending. You and me, we already know the real ending. This is just an ending I made up.

Time passes, Dougherty forgets a lot. Anaheim's gone, Esteban's studio closes, no one's sure why, the Stampfs disappear, Dougherty doesn't practice much anymore. He teaches ninety-three teenagers, postal workers, speed-freaks, hardware clerks, single professional women looking for hobbies, nervous lawyers, skinny lab-technicians, and a novice pro or two, how to play Duarte, Villa-Lobos, Tarrega, Wes Montgomery, Chet Atkins, Doc Watson, Brian Jones, B.B. King, Peter, Paul, Mary, and "Yankee Doodle" in the key of G. He makes money, gains weight, gets tired, and every August moves to Massachusetts where he works for pennies in a pub a former student owns, a change of pace and relaxing. He plays a little studio and now and then a club date—there's always work for a good sideman. It's not a bad life, he thinks, though sometimes he can't sleep and has to walk alone until sunup when he returns to his bedroom and flops for an hour or two before starting over again. And on Sunday he gets lonely, but then everyone does.

One Friday afternoon Dougherty comes home with the entire naked weekend stretched out in front of him and thinks he'll check the cable listings or drive to Crotona where a pupil's in concert at a community college—three Paganini violin and guitar sonatas, a nice kid and pretty fair player though awful nervous—or maybe just nurse drinks at a neighborhood dive where the pianist's a friend and they can talk between sets, when the phone rings and a smooth voice wants to know is this the brother who plays the Whooooole Tone?

"This is Dougherty. I play it all."

"Hot licks, big city! You the who I'm callin'. It's me, Iamblichus."

"Huh?"

"The Pythagoreans, man. Where you livin', under a rock?"

"Never heard—"

"Listen, baby, we're talking fusion. All's one, everything comes together, very spiritual shit, dig? Agent's got us in this burg to warm up Walker. You *have* heard of Leroy Walker?"

"Yeah, I know Leroy."

"Well, the guitar man, that's Porphyry, he bops outa here for lunch, and the brothers, we're all into vegetables, see, but he gets back to rehearsal and starts barfin' Big Macs on Thales' amp and Speusippus' new toga—"

"Speusippus?"

"Apollo's Temple, nine o'clock, one set, no break, we pay time and a half."

"Double."

"Double."

Which isn't half bad for a Friday night. Dougherty gets the address and is about to hang up when, maybe because he's older now or because promises aren't paychecks or just because there's this last clumsy silence to fill, for whatever reason, he wants to know did this Iambli-whozits get his number from the union directory or exactly how?

For a moment there's nothing, then a chuckle and the sound of a hand cupping the receiver followed by a murmur someone doesn't want Dougherty to hear, before finally a voice returns, this time so low Dougherty can barely make it out: "You're Dougherty. They told us about you."

And the phone's as empty as Dougherty's head except for this one fist of memory balled up and drawn back into the shadow of some neuron waiting until Dougherty's loaded his Telecaster, cord box, synthesizer, foot-pedals, echo-plex, Twin Reverb, remote speakers, driven halfway across town to a street he's never heard of before, wondering all the while if maybe this isn't all just a hand-job until, sure enough, down an alley in a warehouse district full of ragged shrubs and delivery vans parallel parked nose to fanny in rows like rats waiting to be piped out of Hamelin, he finds a facade of white plywood columns topped in gilded scrollwork with a fake-o marble marquee overhead where Leroy Walker's name is written above a bunch of fraternity letters and, standing in the stage entrance, pate glabrous, feet bare, gold hoop

big as a buggy wheel in one ear, with the breeze blowing what
looks like a white flannel nightie about his scrawny knees, this
grinning fool hallooing Dougherty as if the two of them had just
arrived at their twenty-fifth high school reunion—one fist of
memory waiting balled up and drawn back all this time to suddenly shoot out from cerebral oblivion like a sucker punch and
cold-cock him with a half-formed, tongue-twisted, spittle-
covered, "Th-they?"

"All we need's your machine gun, baby. Rest of that electron
bomb can stay in the trunk. Man, you really are old, aren't you?
This the way to the brothers."

Well, Dougherty's sure he's seen weirder, though he can't
remember when, but he's just a sideman and doesn't get paid to be
amazed so when Iamblichus starts trying to get a nightie over his
head Dougherty wonders maybe he should have held out for triple
time but figures that if you try too hard to avoid the loonies in this
business you'll end up playing for mothballs in a coat closet and so
does pretty much what he's told and tries not to feel silly about it.
He gets introduced around—Nichomachus of Gerasa on
electronic lyra, Speusippus on goat-skin drums, Thales playing
amplified kithara and ram horns, Lysis of Tarentum doubling on
Fender bass and upright—each one half Dougherty's age and bald
as a baby's ass. They play. And Dougherty knows why they called
him: cause no one else would even bother trying to follow this
stuff Dougherty's not certain is music and sure sounds less
wholesome than noise.

"We call that one 'Planetary Choirs'," Iamblichus explains
through incisors as white and flat as drive-in movie screens. "The
opening chord's what can be dug with the spiritually hip ear
whenever Saturn's big rings're harmonically tight with Jupiter's
second moon."

Which is good to know because Dougherty had mistaken it for a
hot ice-pick jabbed in his ear. "Yeah, well, rhythm seemed a little
shaky there where the 7/8 breaks down into—"

Iamblichus slaps his thighs, guffaws. "Listen at him! The king
of strings is talkin' tempos!"

Speusippus gazes up at Dougherty with the pained eyes and

knitted brow of an eternally patient scoutmaster. "The fourfold integrity of the tetraktys makes possible definite, quantifiable relations between harmonic intervals and meters without any violation of the decad's purity, O my brother."

"For example," Lysis calls over, "you play fourths in three quarter because that's the ratio of the string length."

"With tetrachords, of course, we use second-degree equations."

"All's One."

"We're into integers."

Every bit of which help Dougherty's careful not to thank anyone for, but no matter, cause the whole goofy lot of 'em suddenly break out into kidney-splitting laughter and traipse over to pound him between the scapulae shouting, "You a regular son of the One, flash hands," or "Now is revealed our brother's beauty of spirit," or "Yer oooooooooookay, Dougherty."

But he isn't, he really isn't. When they crank up for the next round of pandemonium—"Chant of the Thracian Magi," Iamblichus calls it, but sounds to Dougherty like a vacuum cleaner—Dougherty has even less idea what's happening than the first time, and nobody else seems to be much better off because Thales keeps flashing him this fatuous smile like that was just the most remarkable riff he'd ever heard even though Dougherty's only playing "Row, Row, Row Your Boat" in rounds hoping this bedlam will soon mercifully end. Which after about an hour it does. They all unplug their instruments, and a bevy of roadies, who are the most reassuringly sensible creatures Dougherty's met since he got here, materialize out of the wallpaper to arrange curtains, push around speakers and amps, stick jacks into anything remotely hole-ish and basically transform this wasted grocery warehouse into a mega-volume electromagnetic hinterland with oriental rugs and a few potted palms stuck about at intervals for someone's idea of a breezy effect. In a few minutes Dougherty hears the crowd begin to shuffle, bang, and murmur its way into the rows of seats. Speusippus squats arranging pebbles in geometric figures on the floor; Lysis mumbles prayers over what looks to be an eight-inch pile of dried navy beans, and Dougherty's trying to feel better: in a sense, each performance is every performance and come tomorrow morning no one remembers a sideman anyway, and so fine tunes to the A-440 fork he carries on his key chain wondering if in Crotona his student's fingers are too stiff to respond to the violinist's rubato which in the allegro movement of the E minor sonata is everything and reminding himself to tell the kid at his next lesson how, if you run hot water over your hands just before going on, that'll help.

But the weirdness here just doesn't stop. Dougherty's supposed to be playing in the warm-up act, but when Leroy Walker arrives in a fox fur coat big enough to mate inside of and escorted by about a hundred white girls in striped leotards, leopard's fang bracelets and very red, very pointed shoes, he gives Dougherty a big grin and wink which Dougherty returns with a nod having worked with Leroy on four or five occasions and found him a pretty complicated affair with two faggy sons in Ailey's corps de ballet and all but six hours completed for his master's in poly-sci at Hopkins, and announces he wants to go first. Well, who's gonna argue? And it isn't that Dougherty gives a fine damn whether he's in the feature act or tagalong, it's just that that wink is about the fourth time tonight Dougherty's felt out of something everyone seems to think he's into, and no feature performer—I mean, not one, never, no way—ever wants to go first, and so Dougherty finds himself veering momentarily close to that precipice of the mind from which unembellished human whackiness looks indistinguishable from complicity, but stops short, realizing this way madness lies, and besides the whole idea sounds a little silly. He'd like to ask if Leroy ever sold the pre-war Gibson arch-top Dougherty once made him an offer on and what ever happened to that midget with the gimp arm sometimes played mouth harp for him, but Leroy apparently intends to walk right onto stage—hundred white girls, sixteen-piece brass section, fox fur coat, instrument cases, roadies, dollies, packing crates and all—so Dougherty slips behind the curtain down a corridor and through an open door to avoid hearing Leroy whose sax player, starting to warm up just now, Dougherty notices is a real blower, the sort he'd enjoy trading licks with on a different night, must be new, but not worth breaking your eardrums to listen to, which if you're going to listen to Leroy you're going to have to do.

Dougherty shuts the door, sinks with a whoosh into a lumpy armchair and finds Speusippus crouched in a corner waiting for him.

"It is almost time. The brothers are honored." The kid's eyes look wet and dreamy and Dougherty wonders maybe he's wrecked, maybe he's nuts, maybe Dougherty couldn't really care less but sure wishes something tonight would happen without surprises.

"As long as the crowd keeps shouting, Leroy'll play forever," Dougherty says. "No rush."

"There's an equation for it. Arrival as a function of applied force against the strain curve at the axis of catastrophe with time constant and the social factor as base. Most of the coenobites never make it in a lifetime."

"Keep practicing. You're still young." Overhead the lightbulb is uncovered, too bright, and Dougherty considers slapping at the switch, knowing in less than two hours he'll be taking in enough lumens to boil his corneas, but the room is a junk heap of makeup-smeared rags, sponges, liner brushes, combs, hand mirrors, boxed costumes, styrofoam cups, heaped ashtrays, fast-food containers, damaged can lights, folding chairs, a chiffarobe, a life-size cardboard stand-up doll of W.C. Fields, an antique gold telephone greasy with cold cream, and, inexplicably, a huge green parrot in a rusty cage that right now announces, "Awk! Fuckeroooooo," so Dougherty figures that turn off the light and your rotting body might be detected in a fortnight by the smell but no chance you'd ever find your way out alive and decides to go to sleep. He snuggles deeper into the chair, lets the pud-thump-bubbledy-bubbledy of Leroy's bass man shudder up from the floorboards into his spine, adds, "There's a lot of luck involved."

"Hah, hah."

Hah, hah?

Speusippus' voice comes closer. "The agent says time's no object. The agent says it may take forever."

"Sounds to me like you need a new agent."

"Soloist."

Dougherty cocks an eye.

"The agent speaks of the miraculous coherence of discrete things. The agent says it will be tonight."

All right, goddamnit, the kid's face is split wide open in another of those gooney grins Dougherty's by now pretty sick of, and Dougherty has had it. He doesn't know what's going on here, doesn't like not knowing. He wishes he were sitting in the dive three blocks from his condo talking to the piano player Dougherty's always thought had this weird way of extending a riff one phrase longer than anyone would ever expect, almost like a peach seed you know you've got to spit but cling to, listening to him ramble on about players and hookers and sessions and road trips and bad gigs and the one time he almost made it, almost, just like they all had, almost. Dougherty wants a cigarette, he wants three shots of Irish, he wants to get out of this loony night-shirt and into a hot bath, he doesn't want to answer any more questions, he'd like to stand up right now, grab his guitar, and march right out of here. He's going to.

Speusippus' hand catches Dougherty's shoulder coming up out of the chair. "They are ready."

"They! They! They! Who in the godalmighty hell are Th—"

SLAM-0! The door flies open, whops against the stob. In comes a bent octave from Leroy's guitarist like a circular saw, an avalanche from his drums, more white girls in striped leotards than a doorway could possibly accommodate, Iamblichus waving his arms, Leroy himself dancing across the floor on one foot, Thales, Nichomachus, two roadies smoking jays and a sixteen-piece brass section dressed in gold. Clatter-bang of falling mirrors, makeup cases, cold-cream jars. Dougherty dives behind the armchair, Speusippus lands on top of him. Somebody slams into the chiffarobe, somebody tackles W.C. Fields, somebody knocks over the parrot cage, and—tinny clang, faint spring-click of the cage door, flutter of wings, scramble of creepy claw feet, "Awk!

Awk! Awk! Fuckeroooooooooooooooooooooooooooooooooooo!"—
well, the bird's got a beak strong enough to crack a marble,
enough pent-up energy to make a volcano envious, one huge
grudge against all those humans who for a dozen years have gooed
and girned and poked and wheedled him, he's loose in here, out to
get even, precisely as a rumble from Leroy's bass man sends a
shiver through the wall studs, makes Dougherty's toes tingle,
and—Oh Christ!—knocks the power out.

"What the bloody—"

"Awk!"

"Aieeeeeeeeee..."

Swat, swat, swat. "That's me, you ass-hole."

"Ouchouchouchouchouchouchouchouchouchouchouch!!!!!"

"Fuckeroooooooooo."

"Oh my brothers, knock the holy shit out of it."

What's to be done? We appear to be approaching an ultimate
moment; at such times do not expect anything to proceed as
planned. If you call up the Bell System repair service, the rep-
resentative will explain to you that during a power outage phone
calls can come into a commercial phone system but no one will
answer because the bell can't ring and the lights won't flash. No
matter, cause Dougherty has just scrambled under what feels like
a trash-heap of plastic food trays, dripping paper cups, greasy
rags, trying to get away from those claws that keep grabbing at his
hair only to have his head bang against something plastic and hard
which in utter disregard for AT&T technology flashes twice and
goes—

"Brinnnnnnnng, brinnnnnnnnng,"

—a sound even more startling than the "ouch, bang-whum-
pus, Awk!, wha-the-fuh," that surrounds him. Dougherty picks
up the receiver, and for no reason he or I will ever be able to
explain to you blurts out, "I-I'm in charge here!"

"Guess again, Dodo."

His hand is icy, his hand is sweaty. He will drop the receiver; he
doesn't. He has one thousand three hundred ninety-four questions he wants an answer to right now. The room has become very
still. He doesn't say a word.

"There's been some confusion," she says. "My boys here, good performers but nobody ever called 'em clever."

Nothing.

"I told 'em, listen, all you need's a player. But this Dougherty—"

"I looked for you at the lost and found."

"—this Doughtery's like God or Mozart or Nazis. You can't teach him tunes. He won't play along. Mostly he's chaos. Where you guys are easy, he lives in a box."

"I called up the Y."

"Fella I knew in Seattle once..."

"Seattle?"

"Booked flights for a private airline then drove a UPS truck. Posh life, really. This guy was cute but a letch. Used to say some people need goodness like the rest of us need food or sex."

"I'm a sideman."

"Nope."

"You left."

"Life ain't fair."

"Why?Why?Why?Why?Why?Why?Why?Why?Why? Why?Why?Why?Why?Why?"

"Because this is close as you'd ever get, because effort would've never gotten you this close, because there's something about the world that just makes things turn out this way, because you're stupid, because you're a jerk, because ain't nobody no place got hands like you, because you're the soloist, because you're Dougherty."

"I have my own place. It has a garage. We could meet for lunch. I'm losing my hair. Do you still chew with your mouth open? I saw a movie with a funny actress in it. Are you calling from a pay phone? Don't hang up, don't hang up."

"You never had much luck, Dodo."

"I need you."

"You need to be twenty-two again, you need to eat more leafy vegetables, you probably needed to know at the beginning of all this what you're just now figuring out, but I don't think you ever needed me."

"People change; there are second chances; some things can happen twice."

"And there can be some great endings."

"You're wrong. You were wrong to leave. You're still wrong."

"Be amazing, Dodo, be more than there is to be."

"I don't practice anymore. I haven't played a recital in fifteen years. These kids don't even know how to—"

"I love you."

"WHY DID YOU LEAVE ME?!!!!!!!!!!!!"

Silence, then, "Let go, Dougherty. Let go." Then nothing.

And for the last time in this story the phone is dead and so almost is Dougherty who knows now that freedom's just an ugly trick to lure you here where you can be crammed, slammed, damned and, wham—he's running. He bounces off two walls, puts his foot in a stomach that groans, pulls a styrofoam cup from one ear, hits his head on the corner of the chiffarobe, slaps the parrot in the goddamn beak, is tripping all over his nightshirt but has his Telecaster in his fist, to hell with the case, and without knowing how he knows it knows he's out in the corridor dashing hell-bent-for-leather toward the fire exit and the last chance he'll ever have to make any kind of choice at all. This isn't the first time Dougherty's been cheated, it may not be the last, but something in his chest feels ugly, and he's groping along the wall for a fire door that he thinks he's found but turns out only to be a fuse box and so keeps moving, thinking that whatever has a way in has a way out, that doorways are made by people and that people can find and open and close them, and touches another smooth metal surface that turns out only to be ditto, but this time Dougherty knows the foolscraziesbullieswindlers won't stop him, this time he's learned what the world's made of and will refuse to play games you can't win, and so keeps moving, aware at last that nightmares end, that people can choose to wake up, that your life is *your* life and no fate, petty malice, twist of fortune, not even love or the half-forgotten ache of a name, voice, taste of hair, the hot smell of her face, not even these can take away—

Dougherty's face blows up.

Evidently the corridor turns a corner here, but as Dougherty

oozes down the wall, just before passing into the nirvana of
unconsciousness, just before allowing his Telecaster to slip from
his grasp and render itself upon the concrete floor two hundred
dollars the other side of playable, with his last glimmer of sense,
he realizes that this surface he's just destroyed his profile on is also
metal and smooth and, more importantly, it's cool. And that just
may mean night air. And that just may mean parking lot. And he
reaches up and, sure enough, there's a knob, and he twists it, and
the door opens, and he crawls outside, and eases himself onto his
belly and looks around and can't see a thing. He decides he's dead,
then he decides, no, he has passed out, then recalls that in Crotona
his student is probably packing up his things now with that odd
hollow feeling you always get when the audience has gone home
and left you standing on the empty stage wondering did it even
really happen and that back in Dougherty's own neighborhood
the piano player is coming off his first set and looking around at
the empty stools and figuring this for another night he'll spend his
breaks sipping tonic alone and that the only reason sixteen-
year-old Dougherty ever bought the Fender Jaguar in the first
place was that he didn't know how to carry on a conversation,
because fate, after all, is only a name we give to mistakes we've
come to love and how did Dougherty forget all this? how did he
forget? and feels the cool floorboards beneath his cheek and
decides to swallow the darkness and disappear.

   "HOOOOOOOOOOOOOO-RAAAAAAAAAAAAAAY!"
No use askin' for justice, Dougherty. There ain't no justice.
   Lights. Screaming. Dougherty cracks an eye; his brain fries.
Toooo much light.
   "YEEEEEEEEEEEEEAAAAAAAAA!"
Banging seats, rumble in the floorboards, hyperkinetic buffalo,
applause. Dougherty's head splits open. Jesus! He eases himself
up on his hands, thinks maybe his eyes are open or somebody's
dropped a probe-light through one ear, and discovers for the first
time tonight that this grocery warehouse is huge, that by some
impossible quirk of misnavigation he's still inside it, that the place
is full of more people than Dougherty's ever seen before in one
place in his life, most of 'em kids, ten-, eleven-, twelve-year-olds,

younger, all going flaming loco, yelling at him, waving their arms, stomping on the seats and, oh God, flashing him those grins, that the stage is empty, that the stage is empty, that the stage—

"MU-SIC! MU-SIC! MU-SIC! MU-SIC! MU-SIC! MU-SIC!"

—stage is empty except for how in the hell did he ever . . . ?

"You the whole show, this the time, hotshot holy man. Ain't no more magic but your hands. We waiting."

Dougherty turns. Iamblichus stands in the stage door, grinning, but Dougherty's not sure now, is it gooney, is it creepy, is it maybe just the grin of someone who knows what Dougherty's always needed to and still doesn't, not even now. Iamblichus starts to close the door.

"Hey, wai—"

And just before disappearing, the slender face smiles a last time, big, full, nods slowly, as if to say, "You're oooooookay, Dougherty," and to mean it, and the door's closed now, and Dougherty's beginning to understand.

"MU-SIC! MU-SIC! MU-SIC! MU-SIC! MU-SIC! MU-SIC!"

The feet have got the rhythm and are stomping along. Dougherty gazes across the footlights. Little girls with goddamn ringlets and knee socks, a real fat kid in a sailor suit, two twins slobbering on their shirts, a pimply twelve-year-old trying to smoke, and a tall brother dragging his sister by the hand looking straight ahead like a man on business. Tiers on tiers, row after row of 'em, standing up on their seats, hailing him like a daddy returned home, but for what and from where? Here's no finesse, no silk tie, no Ramirez floating on his knee, no linen program, no one to appreciate what he brings, nothing fine at all, just this messy business of life where all things come too late and find you no longer ready, standing in the center of your own dream in a fool nightshirt with an electrified two-by-four in your fist and six skinny steel strings on which nothing lovely could ever be played, here, at this test of the vitality of a man's delusions: will you do it now when there's nothing any longer to be gained? Will you do it now just because, such as things are, this is going to be your only chance? Will you do it to say death wasn't the only reason? Will you do it for children?

Of course you will. Dougherty takes the Telecaster, slaps the dust from his nightshirt, stands slowly, stabs three times with the jack at the nearest amplifier, finally plugs it, drags the drummer's stool center stage, positions his left foot on the cowbell, leans forward, licks his lips, looks out over the braids and pustules and cavities and sticky fingers and damp eyes, infantile bedlam, and pauses, just a second, as miraculously the whole cavernous place becomes quiet, and says: "From Bach's second violin partita, in D minor, Segovia's transcription, the . . . Chaconne."

A world away, at the end of Dougherty's arm, a hand strikes the D chord, shatters earth, sky, rivers, trees, buildings, truth, hearts, melts away from its wrist, vanishes, as Dougherty leans into the music, floats out on the light and air, and becomes Dougherty at last.

And the story ends here. Not because nothing else could happen, but because I couldn't tell you what it would be. My eyes won't go there—maybe because I know they'd never come back or because, like you, they're afraid there is no such place, or just because we've all grown so weary trying to keep beauty alive. But you should know that this has been a story of goodness and that here at the end Dougherty realizes what every soloist comes to understand eventually, that Jesus died never knowing he was anybody's savior, and so doesn't bar, lets go, and is already halfway into measure two-seventy-eight, then -nine, then finished, and will never be able to remember whether this one time he sharped the C or not, will only know that after he condenses back into fingers, flesh, muscles, tendons, as he flows up the veins of his arm and re-congeals inside his head, he will listen for the applause that doesn't come, will only find stillness and strange eyes, will never learn the meaning of any of this, will unplug his Telecaster, walk to the edge of the stage with his soles making faint squeaks on the polished floor as the crowd remains as silent as earth poised for Armageddon, will jump off the apron into the embarrassment every performer feels at his own unreality before the world of listeners, and landing in the aisle will stride out of the auditorium as children turn their heads nervously to watch him, cutting their eyes toward him as he passes, whispering, stirring, will cross the parking lot, climb into his car and, sitting beneath stars that make no music, with even now no sound or movement from the dark warehouse, here poised upon the nether lip of his own dream, will wonder: if everything was for this, was it worth it? was it worth it? and won't be able to answer.

APPLES

For you, O Strange One, come to us from a foreign country, full of grace.

"You're blind. BLIND! You treat your own son like... like..."

"The play is scheduled for a very short run in Bonn. Everyone is tired of Schiller now. Once we open in Freiburg I'll be able to visit."

"Comme un chien!"

"Don't speak French to me."

"Wie Schiessdrâck!"

"I have responsibilities."

"To whom? The teenager? Or is it one your own age this time? I've seen that 'Hedwig.' "

"To myself."

"When are you going to grow up?"

The black fir boughs whip past my windows. The afternoon light is being eaten by the trees.

"If you'll only explain to him—"

"Va te faire foutre! He's in his bed. Tell him yourself."

"Please..."

"Or is it both of them?"

"I'll kiss him good-night, then tomorrow, if you'll explain."

"Can't you see? We are your life."

The road twists, dives away from my eyes.

"I... I can't face him."

"You are a father. My husband. I've been faithful. *Fidélité*! Doesn't that count for anything?"

"He never calls me father. Never."

"We are your life."

"I don't seem to want that life."

"Like a pig, comme le dernier des derniers, comme un sale insecte!"

The Porsche must find its own way down the mountain now. The forest has grown too dark. I am Tell, sure-sighted, the marksman. I am Tell returning home.

So red, so thingly red and round. And shining, too. If you tugged one, just a tad, there at the nether end where the peel tooches out like a sow's bung, if you tugged there, it would snap, drop, go "thock" when it hits, and in the morning when the sky fired you'd find a bruise and, by the seventh day, a cidery stink in the grass. IT says you shan't. Still, I've watched them fall. If I chose the "thock," IT would say: before they drop, they're hanging, what's the sound of one hanging? And I'd have to hold to the bear's pizzle so as not to blow away. Of course, she says the creep says I'm foolish, but, Sheol! she couldn't even see the creep till I gave it a sound. Look, she said, as we grazed in the long weeds, a rook! But I only saw everything. A foot! A foot! I still had too much picture. A slithering root! she cried, which was wrong but closer. So I stretched out my finger and made it appear: "Creep." The doves beside her nose flapped their wings. Like I said, she said, but she hadn't; she'd said root. I gazed out across the Pishon and spoke nothing. "Creep," she murmured. But she had seen the root. Still, this one is hanging here, though unsounded, and each morning I can see it when the bear, the earth-pig, and I come to watch these limbs fruit shapely in the first fire. Ruddy and plump, it swags no more than a head above my brow and never shivers when through the leaves day leaps screeching onto my face. What if, instead of "thock," this one chirruped like a tanager? or snortled off to plough for pissants in the cassia roots like the earth-pig? She says the creep says that IT ought to let us know what we mustn't know if IT intends to punish us for finding out, but how can you know without the sound? I wonder would IT let me make one sound for the whole thing: bark, buds, bows, sap, and hairy clusters where the wasps lollop? But then, where does all of anything end? Even so, next time IT blows, I'll try to ask. She calls IT air. I tell her: the sound for blowing is not "air." She calls IT air. But pendant above my nose, more lurid than a tongue, as round as night's nipple, and so thingly it cannot be said at all, this uberous gob seems to bloat me with unspeaking, and I know all the air will be gone soon. The bear is growing restless. Perhaps we can gallop over to the Tigris at the edge of the garden and pluck pomegranates, or gaze off toward Cush until the cooling of the light. If only I could fill my head with darkness. So red, so thingly red. And round. Great Tiamat upon the waters, one sound would be worth a thousand of these pictures.

Halfway down Feldberg's slope, just where the footpath joins the rubble road to Todtau, within sight of the amber windowpanes of Frau Rickert's cottage, Martin Heidegger stops. Of course, he must tell someone what he has seen, someone in authority, a bailiff or constable, but how would such telling be? The windburned pupils of his eyes distend, gobble the black fir boughs pinioning the moon. Beneath a harsh light in a clamorous, unfamiliar room, how to speak what lies so silent upon the karakul mat of a rude ski-hut's floor? In what could such telling and this having seen and that which is so boldly there upon the mountain—in what could these agree? He shakes his head, sighs. No, he has seen nothing yet. Wearily, he turns and retraces his steps up the Feldberg.

MALUS Mill. Apple. Rosaceae. About 25 species of small much branched, deciduous trees or shrubs of N. Temperate Zone; sometimes treated as subgenus of *Pyrus*, from which distinguished by pubescent leaf surfaces with acute rather than callous-tipped margi-

nal teeth, broad, pubescent or tomentose winter-buds,
flower clusters prevailingly simple without a columnar
simple stalk, pome lacking stone cells or grit cells,
calyx tube open in flowering and not closed about the
styles, which are more or less united basally. Most
important species are various descendents of *Malus
pumila* ... the wild or original Apple.

I am all eye and fruit's food tonight in this flat above Lake
Michigan, but if you listen, I will tell you what apples can do.
Thirty-one verdant, red and ocher *Mali* shudder upon my window ledge, humming softly in the moon's silver light. If you have
believed in the innocence of medlars, quinces, loquats, it is only
because, like Mariana, you have never been gifted with terror. Be
filled.

"A still life like this one doesn't even make an attempt to be
realistic," she said, gliding along in that half-drowsy fashion of
hers, one finger extended, now toward this now toward that, like
an opalescent snake. "That's characteristic. There's almost
always a self-consciousness about his painting. Look how artifi-
cial the arrangement is, the basket propped on edge like that, or
the way he's scattered the fruit . . ."

Perhaps in Aix, in the steamy Provençal afternoon, green and
yellow were only colors and an apple the hardy reminder of a
fubsy tart's copious haunch. I pull my blankets to my chin, wiggle
my toes to be certain I am still connected. Perhaps there, when
you looked at an apple, you didn't get invaded by red. I can see
their skin's gory moon-sheen dented by the little pits and stems,
the omnivorous shivering of their meaty pomes. I am speaking of
terror, now, not fear.

"Have you ever seen the 'Bedroom at Arles'?" she asked, starting away. "Or this ghastly Hodler?"

I didn't move. "They're just apples." But they weren't and
already I knew it.

"Maybe it's ungenerous, but I always think of the 'Bedroom' as
a very psychotic painting."

Perhaps, at first, it was merely the way the left corner of the table sort of tumbled into my lap, so that I couldn't really believe the apples would stay there, or maybe it was the parallelogram all at once twisting out at you or the cloth plummeting over the edge.

"Come along, David, I want to look at the Rousseau on the end."

"There aren't any curves." But there were and that wasn't what wouldn't let me follow Mariana. I had watched the spheres becoming corners, seen a rising unexpectedly swell or a circumference suddenly fold under, had been startled when a brush stroke metamorphosed into light, but something much stranger was beginning to happen.

"Oh, you mean his outlines. He paints instead of drawing them. Let me show you the 'Bedroom,' " she smiled patiently, "then we can take our time at that Rousseau. Up close, Rousseau's outlines disappear entirely."

But it was too late, for I had already gazed at that dimensionless point where perception was being bartered and had seen what would lead them down State Street, past the doorman and concierge, up the letter chute, the fire wells, the elevator shafts late at night, and perch them humming here upon this sill—what would never again let anything be the same. I leaned forward and with my hands deep in my pockets dug my nails into my thighs. I could feel the sweat beading on my neck. It was awful.

"David?"

And now there are thirty-two.

Running in the hallway, the clamor of heavy shoes, voices approaching.

"...and see if Jaeger has any family in Freiburg. But call his hotel first." Loud knocking. "Frau Konegin?"

"I think he has a son in Altdorf."

"And call the girl's apartment. Weiss, Weiss...Pater knows her given name."

In the forest she had no name.

More knocking. "Gnadige Frau? Anna?"

"Maybe she's downstairs in costuming."

"The girl?"

"Frau Konegin. I saw her come—"

"If you can't get an answer, drive over there."

"To costuming?"

Knocking again. "And get the stand-in on the phone, the blonde one." Footsteps.

"What's her name?"

Receding.

"Ask Pater! Ask Pater!"

Silence.

Anna Konegin rests her hand on the peasant's bodice lying on her dressing table, gazes into the mirror. Nothing was named, only the red fruit, the livid snow, the forest surrounding the three of them like an ebony frame.

Martin Heidegger leans upon the lateral bough of a wind-dwarfed beech tree, listlessly stomps blood into the sluggish veins of his feet. Common sense, he thinks, wants merely to be useful, to do and be done with. From here he can see the undulant black basin of the Wiese and to the north an occasional light on the western shore of the Titisee. His ski hut is scarcely a hundred metres further up the path. Common sense would turn aside. He glances back down the Feldberg. To be useful, yes, but to be used up, to dispose of in speaking... Tyranny of the self-evident! Martin Heidegger pushes off the beech bough and continues up the path. Go. Look. Wait. It appears.

> APPLE—word from root "ap" ("ab") + ending "le" ("ala"), apparently a diminutive form. As used in Northern Europe, yields "ap" ("ab" or ball or eye) + "ple" ("pol" or Baldur), thus eye of Baldur, sun god. Welsh is "aval," thus Avalon, isle of rest, is Apple Island. Source of Apollo, Appleby, Appuldurcomb, Appold. APPLE OF THE EYE—the pupil or circular aperture in the center of the eye. Symbol for that

which is cherished with highest regard. The apple is
not mentioned in the Biblical account of THE FALL,
and some believe an ear of wheat, a fig, or grape may
have been intended. Possibly a Semitic word for fruit
was translated into Old High German "opaz" or
Anglo-Saxon "ofet" both of which may be rendered as
"apple." Celebrated in FOLKLORE & MYTHOL-
OGY as a means to immortality, an emblem of fruit-
fulness, an offering, or distraction in suitor contests, a
cure, a love charm, a test of chastity, a prize for
beauty, a means of divination, a magic object, and
according to VOLTAIRE'S STORY OF NEWTON, as
responsible for the discovery of the law of gravity.

*They are out there but the sound is in here. Then you make the
sound, and the sound is out there but they are in here. The sound
is like your mouth. When the sound eats them, they are in here,
but IT says your mouth shan't. I am as big as the biggest sound I
make. IT can't be eaten. Eat, she says the creep says: you make
sounds because your mouth is empty. But what would be in here
if I ate one? I know red, the raggedy-edged craters where the
aphids wriggle in, the vinegarish stench, their quivering blankets
of sucking flies. I know the blossom's hum, the trunk's nubby
skin, and the "thock" I didn't hear but knew had sounded when,
before the sky fired, the bear, the earth-pig, and I came to graze
and found this new one here in the grass. Eat, she says the creep
says, and you will have pictures. But when IT blows I realize I
must have sounds, and afterwards, if I ask the bear, he only
yawns and acts as if he doesn't understand. She says that the bear
is bored with IT and that the cats think IT's vulgar. The earth-pig
plumps his muzzle in the milkwort. She says the creep says air is
air. I say the sound for blowing is not "air." But staring at this
purple bruise I never heard "thock," not touching—IT says you
shan't—I am all picture and already long for the light to freeze
and night's nipple to suckle my head. Even then there are pictures. Maybe IT would accept a combination: "pendant-*

shapely"? "hanging-sour-'thock'-shan't"? Sometimes when IT
blows I can't make my sounds. My hands become river, and if I
squeeze the bear's pizzle too hard, he goes off to sulk in the gorse.
But to fill with IT's wind is too horrid if not soundly, and once I
had to gallop away toward Havilah to low loud where even the
weasel wouldn't hear. I lowed until I saw night's nipple and lowed
until the fire and lowed until I slept in the mud by the stiff-weeds
and woke empty. The sound for blowing is not "air." Sometimes I
think I could just pick up this new-"thocked" one, put it here
under this front leg I don't use much anyhow, and when she
needed the sound, I could hold it in my paw. It would be out there
but the sound would be in her and here. But would it? IT can't let
us know what we mustn't know, I explain, until I make the sound
for what IT intends to punish us for finding out. She only laughs
and gallops off to loll with the cats in the mimosa. Sometimes I
wonder if she even hears IT. She claims she does, but I'm not sure.
I've got to make the sound soon, or when IT blows, I will blow
away. Eat, she says the creep says, and IT will be your picture.

Not merely that the girl never loved, thinks Anna Konegin, nor
that his chest and garlic breath, the meaty gnarls of his
huntsman's thumbs, not that these failed to bring us as much to
each other as to him alone, but that silence, my silence, was too
sublime for them.

For us.

She lifts the greasy peasant's bodice and, staring, shakes her
head. The treachery of names. Who would have thought, having
been christened with grace, I'd end such a queen?

Once upon a time they'd come together in a small room beneath
the beech boughs, had mingled stench and grope with the forest's
fusty spoor, had clacked teeth above the girl's livid throat until
their minds felt venomous, clear. How then could she have
dreamed of a meal of liver and lungs, of the mirror's doggerel and
the poison fruit? Having momentarily sloughed performance,
living at last in the dark nothing of her emptied self, even then

Anna had noticed that the girl's hair was black as the Schwarzwald, her skin white as the Feldberg's ice, her lips so crimson, and perhaps this should have been her first warning that equivocation was at work.

Anna tosses the bodice into a hamper at one side of the veneer wardrobe. But, as he would finally insist, they were actors, and once he had assumed his role, once the girl's pale buttocks and nude feet had glided away across the crust of ice, then it was no longer possible to shuttle between perform and be. No more Anna, no more Hedwig Tell, only grim Konegin feeling old, old.

Footsteps approaching, knocking again. "Frau Konegin, Anna, we know . . . we think, probably, you are in there."

Calling from down the corridor, ". . . Bond . . . ?"

"We have one hour and a half until performance, and no Tell, Anna, no Berta. We are . . . I am desperate."

Coming closer. "Herr Bond?"

"We can, we think, get a stand-in for the girl, but who in Freiburg can —"

Panting. "Herr Bond! We've reached Jaeger's wife in Altdorf!"

"Well? Well?"

"She hasn't heard from him in months. Quite angry, and there's the son, you understand. But —"

Banging on the door. "ANNA!"

" — but the constabulary thinks they have found Fraulein Weiss' —"

"How soon can she be here?"

"Her car. They've only found her car. At an inn near Todtau. Abandoned. Pater called."

"Grosser Gott! What business has she with an abandoned inn?" Rattling the doorknob.

"The car abandoned, not the inn."

"Is there a pass key?"

Footsteps again.

"It wasn't locked."

"Frau Konegin's room! A key to the room."

Receding.

"... saw her come in."

"Ask Pater ..."

"... and the apple is missing..."

Anna opens her wardrobe, shuffles through the moldy crinolines, scabrously painted mock-silk, Spanish shawls, twill sashes, a cheap oriental gown, all the paraphernalia of possible lives. Hadn't she always known the power of names? Why else had she been so insistent on the blackness of the forest, the thoughtless red fire of each kiss, the colorlessness of having been nothing at all? She had believed that there, surrounded by dark beeches, darker firs, that there, surely, fruit was fruit, merely flesh, core, peel, shape, that in the forest an apple could be safely eaten. From the wings they had watched the girl manipulate the gob each night behind Gessler's horse, had seen her pierce the spell of Schiller's play as she pierced the pome, so mechanically, such a matter of fact, seen her place the punctured fruit upon the boy's head, this fatherly miracle become a mundane, sleight-of-hand, *fait accompli*. No wonders. No surprise. How, then, in the forest, no longer performing, alone, unstaged, how could meaning still poison such homely food?

Rags, Anna, thinks. She slips the shawl from its hook and ripping it along a seam, wipes it in the dust on the baseboard, along the top edge of her dressing-table mirror, dabs it in the sooty corners of the wardrobe, then drapes it about her face. Yes, she had known the power of names, but not their deceit. To have been three mouths, six hands, to have assumed and exchanged and discarded parts—wench/trollop/matron/dowager/biddy/minx/slut, mother and daughter, lord and rogue and victim and queen, QUEEN—to have effaced all memory by so much dark touching that finally one had ceased to be a doer at all. To live in the forest. No, perhaps it was not that the girl never loved, nor the paleness of her youth as Jaeger had warned, nor even—maybe it was not even his lechery for speech.

But who would have dreamed she would end such a queen?

Anna wads the oriental gown into a hump and crams it down the neck of her peignoir until it hunches irregularly above her shoulder blades. She stoops and, in her mirror, watches herself hobble about the room. You take parts, you slip so easily in and out of lives that you come to believe substitutions are endless, then one night in the forest another character, a circumstance, perhaps simply a freak of place and time—a piece of stray fruit—something brings you up, says, "This is your name." Then no more audience, no more faces, no more shadowy wings where you wait. She smiles. Of course, I brought the apple, she thinks; of course, I knew it would poison everything.

> Mirror, mirror, on this table,
> Was ever queen so contemptible?

A loud cackle rises in her throat, fills the room.

"They're moving!"

"Please, David."

"But they won't stay still!"

Mariana peered at me over her menu. "I think we should order now."

"You're going to EAT?"

"David, it's only a painting."

"NO! NO! NO!" The waitress fidgeted at the bar each time my fists hit the table. "They wobbled!"

"All right. They wobbled."

"I saw them."

"You saw them. Now order."

I leaned forward, hissed. "How can you think of food?"

Mariana closed her menu. "You're right. I can't think of food." She picked up her bag. "But I can leave."

I clambered to my feet. "You have to go see them."

But Mariana didn't have to go see them. She only had to smile, a little sadly, take three steps to the door, and disappear.

I had to go see them.

Keep the Rhein to your right. The Porsche will take petrol at

Lorrach. Then across the border and eighty kilometres to Luzern.

When she sees me, when she sees my eyes, she will know. I have left the forest behind. And perhaps he will call me...

>   Wherever general agriculture is practiced, the apple is the fruit of fruits. Temperature is the commonest limiting factor for its cultivation in North America. The apple cannot be counted upon to hold its own in regions where the temperature goes down with frequency to 20 degrees below. Long, hot summers are as trying to the apple as cold winters. Dry weather is another factor. Slopes which give air drainage, irrespective of direction, are better than level lands. Apples will not thrive on sand or muck.
>
>   Careful attention to pruning is required, especially during the first five years, so that the main scaffold branches are well distributed and weak crotches do not break under heavy fruit loads. Most apple varieties should have some fruit 6-8 years after planting. They should soon after bear a full crop and go on doing so for 40-50 years.
>
>   At this time they become what the foresters call over-mature. If you have a place with old or over-mature apple trees, you will have to come to a decision about them. They are picturesque, even beautiful in blossom, but generally not much good for fruit. A process known as renovation involves cutting back the old branches as much as one third, or one half, in order to force out young wood. Few commercial orchardists think the labor is worthwhile. As a practical matter, such trees should be destroyed.

Martin Heidegger studies, reflects upon, perhaps only looks at the woman's body lying east-southeast on his karakul mat. Nude body. Nearly nude body. He decides it is neither thoughtful nor revealing to say she is dead. She may be asleep, frost-bitten, overcome with exposure, exhausted, faintly breathing. Did she come here under her own power? Are we considering a question of will? Moreover, why call her by what is for this place, this time, least essential, least here? In all this, where is *she*? We are regarding the inessential, the changeless, the necessarily indifferent. Death has not appeared yet.

Slowly, Martin Heidegger steps across the body, glances discreetly, then turning his face, more boldly, at the branch of odd leaves tied by—is it a clematis vine?—to her waist. Why speak of this as "woman"? Does "woman" presence her upon this mat? What is "womanly" in this splayed thigh, slack mouth, back-bent elbow and akimbo hand? How is this fleshly pallor, this dark-making lividness, "woman"? Is this mere function, *in potentia*, or history? Is man manning here? Nothing is seen.

In potentia! Martin Heidegger scoffs. No, we are not concerned with abstract correspondences, with *veritas est adaequatio rei et intellectus*. Where is "womanly"? This is *corpus*, stuff, body. Martin Heidegger lowers himself into the straight-backed chair beneath the cracked kitchen window. Body is lying upon the karakul mat on the ski-hut's floor. Darker still. Chair is body; plank is body; teacup is body. She, *she*, is not body. Body does not persist in this open. Earth will not rise up under it. The fir boughs cannot frame it. Where is its sky? Nothing dwells thingly in this bodily seeing. He runs his eyes up the arch of her foot, over her leafy hip, along her crooked arm. How to establish such— Stops, leans forward. In her hand, between her fingers, something, red, yes. . . . He peers more closely. And from one side, two bites.

IT is too big to be eaten. Picture is too hot for my head. The sound is like your mouth. If I had IT for picture, my picture would eat my head. Sometimes I wonder, maybe she is right. She told me that, when she squats to make mud, she thinks I am wrong about sounds. Maybe knowing is what happens then, she said, squatting, as the mud slides out. I watched her but said I did not know like that. She laughed and said, no, I didn't, but she did while making her mud and maybe I could while I made mine. I don't know. I've watched her drag her claws through the cat's fur, and

*she smiles then like she has the sound. But then where is my
picture? The bear can have night even while the sky fires. The
earth-pig grunts too tunely to know if he knows at all. I wonder
why the creep never speaks to me? Maybe IT can't be eaten
because IT is not picture. Eat, she says the creep says, and you
will know.*

I would leave my office early each afternoon, catch the el at
University Station and be in the loop by four, four-fifteen. I
wasn't being followed then so I didn't have to worry about staying
after dark. The first few times I tried to act very natural, made a
point of strolling through other rooms first, even disciplined
myself to walk past it once without stopping. Then I would time
myself: forty-five seconds in front of the Seurat, fifteen before
Picasso's guitarist, another twenty or so at either "The Water-
fall" or Matisse's "Woman before an Aquarium," and, if the
guard was the same as on the previous day, I would always — just
to confuse issues — take out a pad and pen, stride over to the
"Moulin Rouge" and abruptly scribble something down. I tried to
sustain this for a full minute. Then with a satisfied jerk of my
head, as if I had completed the important business, I pocketed the
pad and pen, loosened my tie and took up my position.

Some nights a whole hour or more would pass before I began to
see them. Once I got my first glimpse just as the guard poised his
hand above the light switch and began coughing irritably. Other
times they seemed to meet me before I even planted my feet
firmly, as I was raising my head, seemed to lunge forward. Oh,
there was nothing tame or courteous about them. Sometimes in
the dark doldrums before my eyes had taken hold I would inspect
their surfaces, wished I were allowed to stroke them, thought
about how savage and tactile they seemed. Occasionally I even
counted: thirty-one, thirty-two, thirty-three. But once I had
begun to see, once they had started shuddering upon the canvas,
had begun their potbellied waddle toward the table's edge, then
the terror was everything and no time remained for refinement or
thought.

Soon I found I could no longer be discreet. Immediately upon entering I started toward the painting, never glancing at the Monets and Gaugins as, barely restraining my urge to sprint, I rushed around the corner and nearly dived at the heavy frame, the hideously crackling cloth, the lopsided table and tumbling fruit. That knowing was the worst, I believe, for despite all the indications—my perverse need to see them, the impetuosity that I refused even to acknowledge, and the way they hung so crassly there, careless of their own brute life—despite all these warnings, I still believed in their innocence, my self-possession, in the safety of just looking. If I thought at all then, I must have sensed that more was involved than ordinary fear, that mere fascination seemed too light, too playful, but it wasn't until that first evening, moving through the damp night up State Street, thinking only of my supper and bed, trying to empty my head of its strange fatness, that wordless sense of being overcrowded, too full, it wasn't until then, as I first gave in to that almost unadmitted impulse to glance behind me, to see only shadowy figures, the dim walk, the garish signs and taxi lights, it wasn't until then that I knew I was no longer in control.

I returned to the Institute several more times, but gradually began to avoid the downtown loop stops, would ride up to the near north side and walk back or would get off as far away as Sheridan or Jackson Park. Once walking home I saw a cheap print of them in a store window and, without ever thinking, ran inside, paid the clerk, seized it and barely got outside again before smashing it into a pulpy wad. I thought of returning, just to reassure myself that they were still there, that they had not moved or changed or that there were not fewer of them somehow, but always when the time to go arrived, my nerve failed. Besides, I reasoned, they would be there; they would be there because I was.

For now I was being followed. Behind hydrants and the tires of parked cars, in abandoned doorways, sometimes with their stem-less nodules almost poking above an upraised curb or storm drain, always rolling out of sight, disappearing into shade, but allowing me, not quite a glimpse, but something more certain, a sense of their departure, their abrupt absence, their clumsy waddling away. And I would be left there, staring at nothing, my eyes full of green, yellow, and red, red.

"David, I care about you a great deal, but—"

I didn't tell Mariana everything, but I told her enough. "Then take me away."

She sat a long minute watching me, then bent toward the coffee table for a cigarette. "Where?"

"Anywhere. Some place north where it's cold, colder." I wanted very badly to sound reasonable. "Or just away."

"Are you talking about getting married?"

"I don't know. Yes. I suppose."

She stood up and went into the kitchen. "Drink?"

"No."

"I suppose I don't really understand." She came back to the couch with a tumbler of grapefruit juice, lowered herself into the crook of the arm. "I really want to understand, but . . . I mean, if it . . . bothers you so much, why don't you just stop going there?"

I shook my head, tried to smile. "Too late."

"Can't you just forget?"

I looked at her, didn't speak.

"You'd have difficulty getting a job like—"

"I know."

She took a long swallow from her glass, then blurted. "I have seen it a hundred times, David, more than a hundred. I've seen the one at the Louvre, and the one in London with the plaster cupid. It simply makes no sense."

I waited.

"The red ones in the Louvre are even richer . . ."

I waited.

She stubbed her cigarette in the ashtray. "David, do you love me?"

My palms were sweating again. I wiped them on my trousers. "One night the guard turned out the lights and I didn't even realize the building was closing, that it was dark, until he took my arm. I jumped."

Mariana regarded me a long time.

"If marriage seems too . . . too impulsive," I began, "then we could just share a place somewhere. In Quebec, maybe. Or we could still have separate apartments, if you thought—" I leaned forward. "You can't believe how red—"

"I love you, David," she lowered her eyes. "But I can't help you."

And so, that night, the first one appeared at my window, wobbling, humming so faintly I could scarcely hear, swelling in the moonlight until at times it seemed too large for the sill, seemed to hang there in disregard of Newton, and with its sepal breathing noisily, sucking the air from my room. I lay in bed watching its glabrous pits glaring at me, feeling as if there were not enough of me to endure it, as if I were too insubstantial, too light, would explode, be blown away or dissolve. Or be devoured.

Then I understood. Then I realized that terror was not something you felt but something in which you are, that it was like ocean or space or air or field. It took possession and, if you leaned into terror, it would support you. I stopped riding to distant el stops, stopped lurching along the streets like a man pursued. I did not dawdle, but I began to relax again. When the others started arriving, I noticed but was no longer surprised, and sometimes I would let their humming, louder now, lull me into sleep. I thought of the Provençal and reflected, a little scornfully, upon the banality of all that Mediterranean light and heat, but did not reflect long, for I was all there in my room with the knowing which filled me. I was bloated, tumescent with knowing—though until now I had never understood that it was a way of losing, of passing out, of leaving yourself. I looked at gem clips, seams and cuffs, zippers, slats on blinds, dangle cords, my chiffonier, drawer pulls, casters, and wondered, not what they were for, but what they *were*. And always I returned to the humming, the red wobble, my window above the lake. I suspected this could not last but floated upon the terror. I was filling.

Anna empties a hopsack prop bag and, cutting the bag's seam with toenail clippers, wraps the loose fabric about her hips and safety pins it at the waist. She tears the sleeves from a silk blouse

she wore once as a long-suffering Japanese concubine, X's a sash,
bandolier fashion, across her chest, and being careful to muss
every spot of apparent freshness or unsoiled cloth, she stuffs and
ties and drapes sweaters and shawls and kerchiefs about her body.
Sitting, she regards herself in the mirror.

That Jaeger for her, the lackey upon the castle's backstairs,
would be the strutting father of his own tale, his own sure-eyed
hero, and Anna merely his peasant Hedwig, no queen. Or that
white was anything but snow, that it was always at once innocence and vice, and that Anna, in falling for this would play out
the girl's fall too, that such simplicity had gone unnoticed seems
only comic now. She begins to paint her nails, long, red.

"... I don't care what you tell them." Footsteps, a final time.
"Tell them she's ill."

"But they only want to question—"

"Not until afterwards." Knocking. "Anna, dear, I must... I
would like to speak with you."

"They're very insistent, Herr Bond."

"Lie. Offer them money. Go."

"But—"

"Lie! Let them arrest Pater. Give me the key. Now go, dunder-
noggin. Go!" Knocking, softly. "I'll pay bail."

"Y-yes, Herr Bond." Footsteps receding.

"Anna, dear, I know you are there, and I have a key to come in,
but you understand I would not like to intrude." Pause.

The girl did not run deeper into their forest, her pale buttocks
opalescent even in the smoky light of morning, but into her own
forest, the garden.

"Now, Anna, something very distressful has occurred. We... I
am not alarmed, but there are some difficulties. I will explain to
you because YOU KNOW NOTHING ABOUT IT. Afterwards,
I will ask for only the slightest acknowledgment. Do you understand?"

Yes, now she understands why the girl did not come back, why
Jaeger will not come back, why she must traipse the forest alone.

"Of course, you do. Now it seems Fraulein Weiss and Herr
Jaeger have disa—have not arrived yet. We have the Berta stand-

in for Weiss, and shortly Barth, Werner Barth from the Strassbourg guild, will be arriving to play Tell. This will be very pleasing for all of us. We have not spared expense."

To play, yes, but finally to be. Be. Tell is, now, but not here.

"We have located Frauelein Weiss' car. Somewhere in the mountains. A place you WOULD NOT KNOW. Evidently there is some confusion about other cars, two . . . er . . . people—no one knows who, you understand—other cars that were, or lately have been there, at night, with hers. And the authori— the owners of the inn mentioned a Porsche, a gray Porsche. This coincidence is, perhaps, unfortunate for Herr Jaeger."

But now there is no confusion. We each know the other for whom he, she is: the sure-eyed huntsman, the innocent nibbler of forbidden fruit, a wicked, wicked queen.

"Not that there is any reason to suspect, you understand, anything untoward. There are some people with whom you will, we all will, want to speak about this. But LATER."

Anna lines her crow's-feet with the accent pencil, darkens the pits of her cheeks, thickens her brows. Her soft cackle rattles dryly.

"Good, good. Now all I need from you is a small assurance, a word, even a nod of the head will be sufficient, to indicate that, yes, you will be able to play your part tonight, just as usual. Now, I have the pass key, but I would prefer, you understand, not to use it."

Anna tapes the last hump to her nose, and with the pancake fleshes out the seams. All the fables lurking in a name.

"So, I will wait here sixty more seconds for you to open the door and . . . and just reassure me, that everything is . . . you understand, normal. I am only making certain. A nod, one of your lovely smiles, will do nicely."

Anna stands. Someone will be able to tell her where the cottage can be found. She leans upon an old broom handle and hobbles toward the door.

"I'm waiting, Anna."

But who would have thought . . . such a queen?

Martin Heidegger scuttles past the darkened windows of Frau Rickert's cottage and, kicking the rubble with his Swabian boots, passes into the blackness of the fir boughs. The chill of the Schwarzwald night does not reach him. He sees nothing. Word stills thingly, stands before, has brought light into the clearing. He will arrive at the prefecture before midnight. Martin Heidegger carries Being to Todtau.

Monuments have been erected to a few of the most notable apples. In 1895, a monument was erected in Wilmington, near Lowell, Massachusetts, to the Baldwin apple, with the following inscription:

This pillar, erected in 1895
by the
Rumford Historical Association
incorporated April 28, 1877,
marks the estate where in 1793
Samuel Thompson, Esq.,
while locating the line of the Middlesex Canal,
discovered the first Pecker Apple Tree.
Later named the
BALDWIN.

The first tablet in New York State in memory of any apple was erected in the town of Camillus, Onondaga County, on the original site of the Primate Apple Tree. John T. Roberts, Syracuse, New York, on September 11, 1903, caused a bronze tablet to be erected there. On this tablet is the following inscription:

On this farm Calvin D. Bingham,
about 1840, produced the marvelous
PRIMATE APPLE
named by Charles P. Cowles.
GOD'S EARTH IS FULL OF LOVE TO MAN

So I told her to tell the creep about how there was so much fire we couldn't have night until I made the sound. But she said the creep said, IT made the sound and I had no picture. Then I told her to tell the creep how our heads got so big we had to roll them in the oleander. But she said the creep said, even after the sound, did we see IT? And I had to admit, no, but we ate all of the garden with our mouths. But she said the creep laughed at me because the fruit was still out there. I will make the sound, I told her to tell the creep, and the fruit will be in here. Then she galloped twice around the dewberry and said the creep said, IT would not let me. She said the creep said that sound is what your mouth eats when you have no fruit. She lay down beside where the bear was having night in the fire and said the creep said that IT had taken all my pictures. Then she scratched like the cats scratch and lolled on the bear's head and wiggled his pizzle at me. I ate weeds and said I would not listen. She giggled in my ear and said the creep said, eat.

And now, at last, there are thirty-three.

The distant, dull slam of a heavy door.

"She'll freeze!"

Jaeger stares dumbly out the window. "She took the apple."

"Run after her!" Anna pushes him aside and gazes out beyond the three cars at the line of beech trees surrounding the inn.

"I heard her in the bathroom. She was crying."

In the afternoon light Anna can just make out the buttocks, pale feet, and stream of ebony hair gliding over the Schwarzwald's snow.

Jaeger is dressing.

"It's our forest. All we have to do is wait," Anna says.

Jaeger doesn't look up.

"She'll come back for her clothes," Anna says.

" 'The snake,' " he says stuffing his shirt into his trousers.

Anna grabs his sleeve. "Don't say anything!" Touch and know

and the tartness that seizes your gums and nose, a thrill in your
head, the mulch that swallows in a lump—an apple is an apple is
an apple. "Please..."

"In the bathroom. She was crying. Then, she said. 'The
snake,' " he says.

But it is too late, and as Jaeger turns with his hand upon the
door and gives Anna the mad smile, she already knows he is going
to speak. She lets his sleeve slip from her fingers.

"I am Tell."

Her face caves in. "No." She hears the door slam. "No."

The Porsche rumbles, scatters stones.

There isn't enough darkness anywhere in the whole world.

The fog lamps make alleys in the night. The Porsche hums, its
steering wheel warm in my hand.

I will reach Altdorf by midnight.

I have seen one.

Yes, I had seen thousands before, had seen them perched upon
the boy's round scalp each evening in the glare of can lights or,
before that, in the endless rehearsals on hot afternoons, had often
smelled them going sour in the prop trunk, had slipped in the gum
they dribbled on the floorboards, and watched as, so craftily, the
girl—a mere actor—pierced them with the arrow behind the
crupper of Gessler's horse, yes, I'd held and peeled and even eaten
them, as a youth perhaps had watched them dangling in orchards
and shied them at squirrels, but stepping to the mark, as her thin
shoulders stiffened, her chin rose to welcome a badly aimed arrow
full in the face, her eyes disdaining the dark's blindfold, and never
looking askance, pale, blue, blue eyes, no smile, no word—
stepping to the mark, I set the lock, laid the shaft, peered down the
stock at the arrow's horn, the smooth oak stock, and feeling my
finger on the tongue and rolling my cheek over the butt and
muscling all of me into a single eye, I, for the first time and for
everytime, for Time, I saw one. And he will call me...

"You could kick the ball with him."

"Me?"

"You could take him for a drive. Go hunting."

"Are you crazy? I can't even shoot."

"Then just talk to him. You *can* talk."

To have been a huntsman, a man of dank glens and backstairs, a lackey to fulfill the dirty dreams of ladies and lords, to act out boldly what is less than wish but desired, to drive the shaft into a white loin, to spirit away a parent's malformed progeny, to lose a maiden in the wood, the tidier of a family's shady disrepair—a man to do in the night, reflect not at all and to know this black fruit only by my spectator's salivating gawk—to have acted but looked. . . . I will never eat one again. For in seeing her seeing me, seeing us, in watching her rise to our mouths, our hands, in touching the round plummet of her child's belly and the artless dark crying of her need, need, need, in this seeing hadn't I gone out? Hadn't I shimmied up my legs, sloughed off my torso and crammed me into my throat, elbowed and kneed and spined my way along my head until, at last piled up behind one eye, waiting, hadn't I discovered myself empty, spilled out through my squint, somehow gone? Yes, I saw me edging off along the shaft, creeping away toward the point, called to myself perched, poised upon the horn and, too late, felt me spring with the twang, lunge, sail out on the string's hum, slam into the gory peel so that, mired in pulp and mawkishly stodged, I could no longer act ever again at all.

"After I'm gone he'll be relieved."

"Cochon!"

Oh, I was a huntsman, all right, and when instructed by a queen to carry a stepdaughter to the wood, I obeyed, served up liver and lungs as a feast, devoured the white flesh like a kitchen dog, licked her pale hand and waited for my new part, a man prepared unthinkingly to fulfill a dark role. Having never been, what did it matter after all? But now I was to contrive this horror center stage; I who had never looked was to be watched—countrymen, riffraff, logue and boxes, boy, groundlings, Gessler on his horse. This was form's form, the hot minute upon the bare apron, the naked is of do, and I was only an actor, Anna! Only an actor! Yes, I had seen thousands, thousands, but all concealed in their skin, in their fruit, in their seed, in their life, and now launching myself upon the shaft across the forever of space, the demesne where ladies and lords had beckoned me so knowledgeably—"You are a discreet man, and a desperate, and would have a morsel to eat for a night's bit of business, and a drop to drink and something else besides, for a brief night's black affair"—yes, watching myself ravish the airy, pale breast of space, sailing toward her, I felt the tugging of my cheeks, a twitch at my mouth, the first shiver of laughter flutter over my tongue, ripple through my teeth, spill out of my lips, and knew I could not contain myself, because she had said, "The snake," she had called me, "the snake." I had to laugh. I'd never seen anything at all. I notched the string, placed the bolt, butted my shoulder, raised the stock, felt my finger greasy upon the tongue, squinted, waited, sighted, squeezed, heard, looked—but to have known her scarcely pubescent hip in a cold room, to be that chaffing of a father's child's flesh and feel other hands there, another mouth, other breath, to allow that lightless touch to be all, pure presence, to be nothing in the black wood—not even a huntsman.

"You? William Tell? Ça me fait rigoler!"

No, it is not understanding that has brought me back, sent the girl away, given me this name. For lowering the crossbow, as the wind swept down the Feldberg and blew my hair full of the distant lake and the smell of the fir trees and blew away the can lights and the coughing and the barely lit faces in the mezzanine, I had seen nothing and so knew I had become at last. How quiet I felt then. The Porsche hummed down the mountain. Somewhere behind me the girl glided across snow and black limbs. Safe, I thought, safe. Perhaps I worried about Anna, but there seemed little room for worry as the firs whipped by. Time was gone out, and sky was gone out, and the cold bed and lightless room were gone out, and I lay curled up inside the sappy fruit that the girl held sailing over the snow. With my feet entwined about the style, my head resting in the carpel, my arms hugging the sepal and stem, I slept within its dark life where my arrow could not go. And though I knew I would still have to stop at my apartment, conclude affairs, make the crossing of the Luzern in the horrid storm, leap my famed leap, and finally ambush Gessler in the wood, I felt quiet.

Yes, if I could have made Anna understand, I would have said that
this sleeping was sight, this looking out at nothing, and that, in
seeing, you become your name. For I had seen thousands,
    "You'll be the first Tell to shoot your son and eat the apple
yourself."
in market stalls, on sideboards, in galleries, on trees,
    "...No..."
had watched as the girl secretly stabbed them with the arrow each
night, had learned to warn the properties manager when they got
juicy and to recognize one without looking at all,
    "What are you anyway, Jaeger?"
had smelled and touched in the dark, had known their tartness in
my mouth, and the cold feel of their tumid skin,
    "...never..."
had burnished and bitten and heard the taut pop of their peels
between my teeth, had blotted the dribble of sap and grown giddy
from their sour fume, and yes, had eaten last night, had taken my
accursed bite, sucked and chewed the lurid flesh so beautiful that
not even a maiden lost in the wood could resist,
    "What are you?"
for once the shaft had flown, I was no longer a huntsman, no
longer my own hero, the shabby image of a shabbier dream, no
actor playing another's dark life, but was Tell, sharp-eyed Tell,
and knew the dull "thock" of a bolt in fruit, knew how to crush a
serpent's head, and understood that where the eye was sound the
hand would be true, that touch was not touch in darkness, that
beyond the fir boughs was light and, even with the whole village
watching, one true shot could win me a life.
    No, I will not murder my own son.
A Life. So I did not tremble as I raised the stock, did not think, or
speak—no, Anna, it was not speech—as the gawkers huddled,
their gorges rising in lust for this old horror, did not fear as I set
the lock, stepped to the mark, notched the bolt, laid the shaft,
fingered the tongue, breathed, waited, peered over the horn to
see, not her face, not even his face, but only the apple, seed of so
much dark, sweet knowing, its fruit, this promise, saw this alone,
all these stories in a meaty gob, and squeezing the tongue, heard

the twang, the leap of the shaft, the string's song, felt the jolt in my arm, and knew I need never live in darkness again. Never. For he will call me—

The tachometer is steady. After Luzern across the lake to Schwyz and the slow climb to Altdorf.

"Father."

He will hardly be asleep when I arrive.

For I have seen one.

So tonight they all have come. And I am prepared. One has already toppled from the ledge and is wobbling like a plump Dutchman toward my bed. In the window, the others tremble very fast. The humming grows louder.

I think again of the Provençal and all that Cézanne could never have known. For seeing is not the domain of those who make but of us who come behind. I lift the phone, and, dialing, hear a short ring and Mariana's voice.

"They are here," I say.

"Oh, David... You... uh, caught me at a bad time. I really can't talk—"

"It will be tonight."

"Could I maybe call you tomorrow?"

"The red is more beautiful than sight itself, as lavish as touch or be."

"Or whenever. I have company."

"I am full."

"David, please..."

"Welcome it," I say softly. "Welcome it."

"Nice of you to..."

I replace the receiver.

Perhaps I will pluck them from trees, will stuff my pockets and walk beside the Golfe du Lion or will drink cider with a portly cocotte and afterwards lick her sour mouth and lie sweating in the Mediterranean sun and sleep and dream this dream I now am and wake to know I am eaten at last and that my life is in the pome and its redness is me. For if it is knowing that has lined them up here, if knowing has suspended the laws of sense and allowed them to shiver and swell, to drown me in red, has aroused them omnivorous and huge to make me food, to keep me waiting here for the first toothsome lunge, the disconnection that will leave me only knees and torso, then only chest, then arms, neck, and head, and finally only the space in this center, this apple that is eye, if all this is knowing, then I say, welcome it, Mariana. For in knowing of, we increase, and in knowing how, we do, but we are consumed in knowing, and I have come at last to this innocence.

The first one has arrived upon the foot of my bed. Others hop from the ledge to the floor, bob closer, humming their pleasant, soft song. I feel its cool skin against my toes. I close my eyes, slip my head beneath the sheets. That is the difference between fear and terror, I think. No one would unwish terror. I am the warmth of eyesight, the tilt of the table, the tumbling basket, the cloth's spill. Tell Mariana I am fruitful. And be filled.

"Thirty seconds, Anna."

Anna rests her hand upon the door. Of course, she always knew apples were not merely apples. Nothing, not even dark wood, blood, snow, nothing is innocent anymore. Still, she hopes the girl is safe. And that Jaeger, yes, is home.

She opens the door.

"Very good, An—"

A dry cackle ripples into the hallway.

"Ach Gott! Ach Gott!"

If they can only show her the way into the woods.

Sometimes there is no coolness in night's nipple and I have picture of all the things still unsounded and become afraid. I was huddled beside the bear in the dark when I felt the wind beat my cheeks and, in between me and day's cinders, saw something black and silver eating the night. It moved like huge jaws across night's nipple and swallowed the smoke, and it plucked me by my face and tore me from the ground. I soared up and below me saw

*her sprawled on the bear's head and saw me still beside her and
the earth-pig twitching at my feet —all silver in the nightsong.
Then it ate me and I passed into it and it made mud of me in its
loins and oozed me out into the sky again and I fell and splatted
on the ground and lay breathing as the black and silver teeth
chewed the trees and the bush and the river and oozed all back out
again and roared its own fear but without sound, without any
sound at all. And inside my bark I thought that here is nothing I
can ever sound and that when I wake in the sky's fire it may not
even be in here anymore but that, if it is, I will not ever get it out
and, if it is not, then it will have lived only this once. And I felt
very small and trembled. So this morning I have come here alone.
She and the bear and the earth-pig are still sleeping, and in the
first fire I do not look for the new-"thocked" ones but pluck this
one where it swags and try not to have picture of what IT's
blowing will be. For the creep is wrong, I think. We cannot know
what we must not know until IT has punished us for finding out,
but still no darkness can be as horrid as picture. Even if I gallop as
far as Havilah and low beyond the weasel's ears, what will be
blown away will not return, nor what is eaten, nor the light
which will then be dark. The bear will hide, the earth-pig will
vanish, and I will have no pizzle to hold but my own. Could I have
made the sound without eating? Maybe IT tricked me. I will know
even what I shan't, will blow away, but tonight my head will be
cool. The red gob will be in here. Even IT cannot go in here. I am
afraid.*

I eat.

Through sleep as viscous as day-old pudding, a stilleto-like
ringing and the hand that gropes its way to the ice of a telephone's
steel receiver.

"Ja . . . ? Was ist . . . ? Kauf—"

"Brock, here, Hauptmann Kaufmann."

"Wait! Wait!" A cough, the squeal of bedsprings. "Ver-
flucht noch mal! It is three-quarter past twelve, Herr Brock."

"Something most unusual, sir."

"You've found the actress? Injured? Violated?

"I'm sorry to report—"

"Not murdered?"

"I certainly hope not, sir. We've heard nothing of her."

"By Wittenberg Kirche, Brock, what is it you—"

"Doctor Heidegger, sir."

"Doctor Heidegger?"

"Here, now, at the bailiff's desk. Arrived not half an hour since."

"Odd."

"We can't make him out. Thought you might be, you understand, more familiar with the university type. If indeed you would call Doctor Heidegger the university type."

"What has he done?"

"Very little, sir. Walks in, quite breathless, in those...uh... Swabian togs of his—the ski boots, jerkin—"

"Ja, ja. And?"

"Well, comes into the office, quarter past twelve, unusual time to be about, marches up to the bailiff, very grave, very full of something, his manner most grand."

Pause.

"Go on."

"That's about all, sir. Hardly says a word. Just waits."

"Waits?"

"Like we should understand."

"No gestures? No messages? No evidence of strong feeling— fear, guilt, anger?"

"Almost nothing. Just stands there at the desk. Doesn't even look about."

"Herr Brock, I have no notion what—"

"Here, too, sir, so I thought, considering it is Doctor Heidegger, you might want to come down."

Pause.

"Perhaps so." Long sigh, bed springs again. "But he does say something? Hardly a word, but something?"

"Not much help, Hauptmann, sir."

"But something?"

"In point of fact, only one word. Beyond half an hour and only one word."

"And he seems to be waiting?"

"That's it, sir."

"As if you should—"

"Understand."

"Understand." Pause. "Well, Herr Brock, what is the word?"

TRACTATUS CANTATUS

Presto (for mixed chorus)

(women) Here is ev'ry-thing logic'lly possible; these are the limits of all we con- ceive.

(women) Pro- po- si-tions that don't appear sensible, rigorous thought'll con- strue as na- ive.

(women) The world is all that is the case,

(men) See how grammar be-comes tau-to-lo-gi-cal! Watch as the elegant thoughts interweave!

(women) Facts not things in lo- gi- cal space.

(men) Sad- ly e-thics has proven in-ef-fa-ble; still we've discovered how little's achieved.

(women) Doesn't it seem such a shame how lit- tle re-mains to be said now?

(men) The world is all that is the case, facts not things in lo- gi- cal space.

Repeat ad infinitum

(All together now) Ma- the- ma- tics- is su- BLIME!!!

113

A Decisive Refutation of Herbert Dingle's Objection to Einstein's Twin Paradox

or

Gravitas

I am a lover riding south on an el train in Chicago and know three things: weight falls; time is always my own; when we rise, we will rise together. Two boys in a sandlot fling stones as I pass. Across the aisle a black man coughs into a napkin. Someone has scrawled above the window, "Brûlez les prisons!"

Having failed at love, I will be marvelous at thought.

Katherine, do you remember when we discovered Lake Michigan? Early summer it was, one of the first warm days. Already the tiger lilies had begun to droop. We had eaten a trout I'd washed in butter and drunk up the white Bordeaux and had driven along Lake Shore Drive never saying a word. My fingers were greasy. We left the car in Lincoln Park, left our shoes and clothing too, I recall, and were wading into the black water when suddenly I saw it.

"Look!" I whispered. "A lake. Lake Michigan."

"Yes," you said. "We are standing in it."

"In . . . in Lake Michigan."

We didn't want to leave, so we tried to sleep on the beach, but a policeman with a golden mustache made us move. And later he chased us away in my car, too, though I explained we were involved in research.

"Do you know the refractive index of moonlight in this water?"

"Yep. 1.333. You always do your research without trousers on?"

Still, the next morning when we woke, we drove back to the shore, just to be certain. I felt so light walking beside you. You held my hand. Lake Michigan.

"We are not speaking of vectors now, gentlemen, not of Newton's 'force at a distance' — that detritus of Hermeticism — nor of the universal constant's inconstancy, of fields unknown to Petrov, mutual perturbation, or gravitinos. Even General Relativity's acceleration can be disregarded momentarily, and Riemannian geometry as well," I said, my voice as deep as dark water filling up the hall. "The time has arrived to speak of ascent." This afternoon a colleague of mine with very blue skin will question this. And how can I blame him? He is concerned that I am professionally irresponsible. He is concerned that I am a vast confusion of cause and effect, of correlation and contemporaneity, of spheres, of times, of me and you. But when I loved, I sailed out upon my thoughts like a boy upon a pigeon. I did not believe in the fall.

"Gravity! Gravity!" I will want to declare, to shout. "Gravity is pernicious. Do not be grave my colleagues, friends..."

But, no, there will be some coughing, the shifting of hands, eyes which meet my own then, like fish, swim away. The heating fan will hum. After a time I will no longer hear what they say.

Across from me the black man shifts in his seat. He transfers the napkin from left hand to right, crosses, then re-crosses his legs, gazes straight ahead. I have often wondered where these men come from, these men who sit across or in front or even sometimes beside me on trains. They always appear, miraculously, already seated, a stop or two after I have gotten on, newspapers folded tightly in their laps, or chewing absently on wet cigars, or, as now, coughing regularly into napkins. The right hand dangles over the uppermost of the crossed knees, bounces with the train. There comes a slow hauling up of phlegm, not violent or explosive, simply slow. The hand rises, napkin unfolded like a book in his palm, the quiet, faintly liquid expulsion of saliva, mucus, perhaps even blood—the man is careful not to let me see it—then the napkin closes, descends to the knee again, dangles there. Waits.

Katherine, I have discovered that love can make you innocent, that there is a knowing which is less knowledgeable than ignorance, though purer, beside which mere experience appears paltry, mean. The Israelites called the act of love a knowing, and even Socrates considered the philosopher a lover first and only secondly wise, but I seem to have forgotten so much. I was taught that the knowledge of science is scientia's pursuit, not scientia itself, but this afternoon I stood and stared at the perfectly square slip of paper on your screen door and listened to the wind from the lake whistle inside my ears. This experience is just a form of words now, and science is truer than words, and words than the rough wool of your mons beneath my palm. But nothing is so innocent as the innocence of numbers.

So I will count their faces this afternoon, motionless under the pale light with the hum of the heating fan and the odor of tung oil faint and cankerous rising from the table, will count their faces on base ten, then bases three and twelve, will render them coefficients and functions of one another, radicands and sines, but I will not try to explain to them what I know. If you were here, Katherine, I might try. But it is best that you are not here because they wouldn't understand, and I would feel foolish. Percy's skin will be as blue as cold water, and he will try hard to appear to be listening, but, of course, this will only be courtesy. Not that I am ungrateful. I do not want to seem ungrateful.

"...a recent article on the decay modes of the simplest of the fermions, the τ lepton, and its original observation by the SLAC-LBL teams in 1975. But the new particle I am speaking of tonight is in no way akin to electrons and quarks, much less to the fermions, and has nothing to do with this endlessly ruminative passion for populating nature with simplicity. I speak against both adamant and fundament, substantiality and indivisibility. Particle physics, properly speaking, knows nothing of it." My voice, as I spoke in the hall, seemed so firm, so calm, that I suppose I said more than I had intended, was too . . . frank. Still, it was strange to hear the first ones sliding from their seats, moving toward the exits.

"You will search vainly among my papers for analyses of electromagnetic radiation, and particle accelerators will produce nothing." I remember the hall's sweet air and the warmth from the podium light, warmth on my throat like Katherine's hair.

"It is, like Feinberg's tachyons, a particle 'on the other side.' But in this case, not on the other side of light, but of gravity. A kind of anti-graviton."

In groups, with heads shaking, with an occasional embarrassed backward glance. Colleagues, students, a smattering of faces from other departments. I had anticipated this.

"More than an unknown particle, the harbinger of a new force, undermining all of our fixed faith in the supremacy of mass-energy, the continuity of space and time."

For how could I have expected them, not being lovers themselves, to understand flight? Never having flown, how could they now shed years, like gowns, and growing lighthearted, laugh, rise? For, Katherine, knowing in you became all knowing, and all I knew seemed nothing to me then. My thought came to lodge in your hands and, losing touch, could only float away. What were nature's "laws"? Oily cloths, musty rooms.

"I have named it the 'leviton.' "

Sliding from their seats, moving toward the exits, leaving me alone.

I board this train in the loop or if, as now, coming on the Ravenswood from Katherine's, I transfer at Washington Street and seal myself in until I reach University Station. A pill passed down the city's gullet, I bump past other lives, jostle them briefly and am seen, then lose myself in the darkness of Chicago's bowel. Near the Tech and Thirty-fifth Street Station I see a young girl on the back stairs of a three-flat fanning her skirt between her parted knees. We gaze at each other, then I am whisked away. I am not curious what she thinks. She does not wonder at the note I hold in my hand. We are not, will never be, so much person to one another. We wonder only how the other has seen and, for that space of seconds, did we come to rest in another pair of eyes. But I am motion, and as velocity increases, the trajectory of my descent curves less sharply down. I approach Earth forever, do not arrive.

But with you, Katherine, love kept me bound like a ball upon a tether. How far above the water does a seabird wish to rise? Each night beneath fuchsia clouds we tossed off our clothes and, entangling leg in leg, floated in the horned shadow of the Hancock Building.

The policeman with the golden mustache pretended not to recognize us after the first time, though already we understood that his presence there, night after night, just as the nighthawks began to dive, was no accident.

"Excuse me. Uh...wondered if you could help us. Seems we've, you know, misplaced our towels," I said, as he stared, mustache twitching, at my dripping thighs and knees. I could feel your fingers clinging to my shoulders, your nipples like pearl buttons against my back.

"Remember us?" you asked.

The policeman slid a pink pad from his hip pocket and began to write. He smiled. "Research."

"Perhaps they were...er...ah, stolen," I suggested.

"Or, you know, if there's been some mistake," you added helpfully.

He tore off the top slip and handed it to me.

"What's this for?"

He continued writing. "How's the refractive index of the water tonight?"

"I don't think he understands us, David."

"Don't you think you're being silly. If we've done something—"

He tore off a second slip and handed it to me.

"Hey! This isn't friendly," you shouted.

"Maybe he understands math. $g(R) = \frac{\delta\phi}{\delta x} i + \frac{\delta\phi}{\delta y} j + \frac{\delta\phi}{\delta z} k?$"

He cut his eyes at me. "Clever. Keep it up."

"But this is Lake Michigan," you cried. "This is our lake, in a manner of speaking."

" $A\mu = \varrho(r)g^{-1} \dfrac{\delta g}{\delta x\mu}$; $F_{12} = \dfrac{GM_1 M_2}{D_{12}^2}$! "

He handed me the third slip and replaced the pad in his pocket. "That last one, that's Newton," he grinned.

"That's pretty good," I conceded.

"That's fifty dollars. The other two are twenty-five each. Alcoholic beverages on public land; bathing in a posted area; littering."

"Littering? Those were our clothes!"

He strolled away. "Pick up confiscated personal effects downtown, eight a.m."

We drove down back streets and sang Rodgers and Hart tunes to stay warm. I covered myself with a recent number of *Acta Physica*, snuck to my door through the shrubs. You followed in the *Tribune*, the sporting pages (just, you said, for the hell of it), when I gave the "all clear" sign. We lay in my bed and I licked your neck and arms and spine till you began to purr, and we told each other stories—"We are in Nova Scotia and you are a giant, kayak-devouring coca-cola bird"—until our bodies felt as light as the sheets, then with darkness filling my head like warm water and the smell of night in my nose, I lay my hand upon your hip and, hovering there beside you, ascended into sleep.

Oh, if you were here now, Katherine, there is nothing I couldn't tell them, no knowing so recondite that they couldn't understand. I could make them laugh, Katherine. If you were here.

The black man stands abruptly, bends to the window, stares, his forehead tightly drawn, then eases back down into his seat. He is perhaps distraught from his disarrangement in space and time, and I could tell him that his confusion is no mistake. High-speed travel in a loop, either straight out and back or around in a circle, always does things to the world, and what he sees through the window is not the same city he knew when he stood on the ground. But his perplexity is surely much richer than the blue shift of light or the decreasing emissions by caesium atoms. Still, I could speak to him of these things. He would be startled, but once calm again, might find such thoughts comforting. The hand rises, napkin unfolds, the faint liquid sound, then the slow descent to his knee again. I will, of course, say nothing.

I found the writing when I picked up our things at the police station, or later that afternoon, flipping through the pad I keep in my trousers, found it in the margin near some field equations from an article in *IJTP* where the page-ends appeared inexplicably thumbed and mussed. It said:

$$\text{Like Newton's } F = GM \sum_{i=1}^{n} \frac{D_i M_i}{D_i^3} ?$$

In a heavy, cramped hand, and with "Like Newton's" at a different angle from the rest, as if the writer'd had the first thought and then the other later, and I stared at it a long time, without thinking at all. Like, today, your note. The writing seemed to refer to $\sum_{j=1}^{j\,max} \zeta_j = -\omega$ of Petrov's type I, so after a moment I scribbled in the space below,

> Only similar in use of Σ symbol (vector sum), though both cases relative to force among (many) massive bodies.
> Why?

and replaced the pad in my pocket.

Those were the nights we battled with apple puns, Katherine, and stank cider-sour in our sleep, remember? We made supper from muscadines, nectarines, some strawberries you bought on the street, and we floated in the lake amid bobbing fruit. I stretched out my arms and felt pears and limes knocking softly against my ribs, tried to catch their stems in my teeth.

"I don't give A-dam for your temptations, you snake," you gurgled.

"Eve-n so, you'll fall for it." A moon-green Granny Smith floated toward my chin. I opened my mouth.

"You must be out of your tree."

"If I had a pair-a-dice, I'd be willing to gambol on it with you."

"I'll bet."

"Fault," I cried, my teeth clacking closed furiously on a wavelet. The apple bobbed away. "That pun's not upon apples."

"Of core-hissss it is."

We stayed in the water until the last apple had floated from sight—not one of them sank—and then skipped back to our clothes. Everything was as we'd left it, except a pink slip charging us twenty-five dollars for bathing after sundown and a warning ticket for public indecency, with "You're pressing your luck" written on it, stuffed into your jeans. I searched my trousers for the pad and found it, upside down as I had expected. On a fresh page in red ink was added:

> How come you guys don't talk anymore like Michael Faraday? So people can understand you. None of your business "why." You think cops are morons? Explain to me the universal gravitational constant.
>
> You and the girl better watch it. Public ND is an ugly charge.

I regarded this a moment, tore the page from the pad, then scribbled at the bottom,

> Forget Faraday (a mathematical illiterate). Forget GM_E/r_E^2, too, for that matter. General Relativity says the acceleration isn't downward, but up. For all the good it'll do you, the gravitational constant (G) equals gr^2/M_E which numerically comes out pretty close to 6.7×10^{-3} (cm)^2 / (gm) (sec)^2 as measured with a cavendish (which see).
>
> You wouldn't really charge us with indecency?

and impaled it on a nearby sapling. Then, gathering our things we hooked arms, and humming "Funny Valentine," started up the beach.

Katherine, was that the night when first we flew? I don't recall driving home. We'd felt our weight fall away before, gazing at each other, had grown lofty, and laughing, had begun to rise, but I believe that night with your hip beside mine and your hair twisting like a draughtsman's curve about your neck, with our heads thrown back, your smile as thoughtless as a new moon, that night our gravity left us entirely, and thinking thoughts of only the lightest weight, we rose over Lincoln Park until our heads were in the clouds, felt the cold air beneath our naked arms, and turning westward above the rose and ocher lights of Sheridan, floated home.

It is a truth of physics that, in moving up, things move away, that space bends outward from the Earth, and in the universal expansion which is life since the bang, things which rise, shed weight, gain mass, and so, accelerating continually, become heavier and lighter at the same space, in the same time. Dicke claimed that nature has a history and, like ourselves, becomes, but Einstein knew that all things travel as straight as possible, there is a warp in space but no weaving, and that though the universe expands, atoms and galaxies never do. So, if in rising we came together, or in coming we rose, then we were galaxies, or better still, moons breaking out of orbit, satellites sliding along the curvature of light like my bony hand along the smooth, dark depth of your curving thigh. There is a frivolity of space, a lunacy which wishes not solely to shed light but to be it, to lighten, levitate, and so rise. Therefore, Katherine, what I am saying is that, though living on Earth, hearts need not grow heavy. Relativity assures us there is no force driving the apple to the ground. Only shells of slower time. Enshell with me and, looping here, we will dress ourselves in numbers, than which nothing is more light, and though our bodies be pinned to this wall of space, we will draw near the speed where here'n'now elide, and, growing younger, our hearts will rise, will rise.

"Has no one considered where this gravity will draw us? Newton's *gravitas* was always a burden, like pregnancy, but because gravid, considered fecund and so, benign, but *gravare* led to grief, to heaviness of heart as well as loftiness of style, and thus the grave, *graf*, which lurked like a Saxon troll in the shadow of the word, was dug, our names engraved there, and so, perpetually weighed down, soon were *begrófon* beneath the universal attractive force in the sexton's spadefuls of earth.''

Rising, they were rising from their seats, stalking up the aisles, leaving. Friends, strangers, turning their eyes oddly downward, as they will do again this afternoon, as Percy will do, as if embarrassed for the pitiful blueness of his neck and jowls.

"This is not the Inquisition, I assure you." He will attempt to smile, but his lips will appear like beached salmon twitching on his chin.

That's what they said to Galileo, too. Or rather, "This is not the Spanish Inquisition," then locked him up for eight years at Arcetri. Maybe Percy recalls this, because his sobriety immediately returns.

"Please, David, sit down."

Götter will be an eigenvalue and Parmel a constant, and Bethge the coefficient of . . . of . . .

I will not tell them what I know.

I know it is a napkin because it is too large for a handkerchief (the man coughs into no more than one fold of it) and coarse like linen, recently starched, without the stiffness of cotton. When he lowers his mouth into the small pocket it makes in his palm, the corners reach almost to his ears, and when his hand returns to his knee, the tip swings and sometimes touches the toe of his shoe. Perhaps he is a waiter somewhere and steals these napkins regularly from the linen cart. But no, this would be an unpleasant thought, the association of this damp cough with food. Still, the possibility is there. I never see these men, with their folded newspapers, soggy cigars, or, as in this case, napkins, when I ride in the mornings. Waiters work at night and so would sleep late. Or perhaps he is the doorman, and the napkins are stolen by his daughter who is a waitress there. Or better, who is a biochemist and comes there to eat with her lover. Yes, when they enter, she hardly acknowledges the man in his uniform at the door. This is a protocol that has evolved over years. The young gentlemen who accompany her never know the man's name, though after a time they notice the slow turning of his eyes when they enter, and perhaps the muted, scarcely intelligible clearing of his throat. They would be startled, even amazed, a little embarrassed, to learn that he was her father. But each time she leaves, she crumples her napkin into a ball, and on her way out, while stepping into the cab he has summoned for her, just before he closes the door, she extends her hand, and as if slipping a quarter into his fist, deposits there a tightly wadded napkin. He nods, closes the door. Her lover diverts his eyes, asks no questions. The taxi drives away.

I do not know this section of Chicago. I do not know this black man. I do not know what draws the paper to the comb.

"I was led to my conclusion by certain elementary observations. First, the odd fact that gravity is the weakest of all natural forces. There is an uncharacteristic extravagance of nature here. To create something as massive as, say, Sirius, only to exert so little influence seems uncanny. The extremity of the case of black holes is, I believe, a confirmation of, not an exception to, this truth.

"Second, a growing conviction that General Relativity's 'freefall' is simply a verbal convenience to facilitate the theory's coherence. 'Free ascent' or even 'universal stasis' would be, from a strictly logical point of view, just as appropriate.

"Third, a new assessment of the significance of Hubble's discovery of the expanding universe. The 'Big Bang' has become for me of late as suspect as the school masters' *creatio ex nihilo*. A speculative extrapolation backwards in time to explain what, to present ignorance, is otherwise inexplicable.

"Fourth, something happens to a man when he falls in love..."

Percy will repeat these words to me this afternoon, though I can still hear them, rich and clear, flowing from my mouth into the not-yet-empty hall, will repeat them with a cough into his fist and the squirming of his eyes, will ask me what they mean. As if their meaning were not as plain as speech could make. As if meaning were less than all that could be appended to a word. And I would do my best to explain to them, if I thought they were young enough to listen, but all I will be thinking is: Why don't they laugh? Why don't they laugh?

"Can we get you some water, David? An aspirin?"

I tried to tell them, long ago, that time does not belong to physics, that there were forces to which even geometry had to bow, but they were always too busy to hear me, stood smiling with their lips as their eyes walked away. I understand. Time is a function of change, and when gravity slows wit, clocks speed. Still, they should not have been surprised. If massive bodies can alter caesium vibrations, bend light, convolute the path of a star, then, Katherine, with you I was set free in time, rolled over its back like a child in a wagon. I pinioned the moon on the Hancock's antennae and, floating in the water, wrapped midnight about my thumb.

"It is December. It is the first snow. It is New Year's Day." I cupped your toes beneath my palm and paddled toward you until my forehead touched your knee.

"It is August," you called back, "my birthday, only I am a year younger this time."

"It is April nineteenth, the sixty-third day of the worst blizzard to ever strike Chicago."

"Everything is encased in ice."

I dipped my mouth into a wavelet and spewed warm water over your back. "And we are not even cold."

"I'm cold," you said scrambling among our clothes for your shirt. The policeman with the golden mustache lowered his flashlight, stepped from behind the stonework. He came toward me like a fat man on an after-dinner stroll.

"And they tell me, lady, that the air in those jail cells is nearly freezing." He turned to me, twitched his mustache. "Do you know what the refractive index of air is at freezing?"

"1.00029. You aren't going to charge us?"

"With PND? Not if you can get into your trousers before I get this ticket written." He pulled out his pad.

My shorts came flying at my face. "Hur-hur-hurry, David!"

"Now listen, you're not really a cop."

"Hur-hur-hurry!"

"Usually takes me about seventy-five, eighty seconds to get

one of these written. That means you got, oh, say fifty-two, -three seconds to go."

My trousers wrapped around my head. "I'm hurrying."

"You think I don't look like a cop?"

"What's Poisson's equation for determining the gravitational potential, φ?"

You began running my belt through the loops. "Pl-pl-please, David..."

"Oh, that's too many for me. I don't speak math, remember? Looks like ten, maybe twelve seconds."

"Then something simple. Kepler's third law—"

"Snap this!"

"Three, two—"

"I'm dressed."

"He's dressed! He's dressed!"

The policeman grinned, ripped the pink slip from the pad, held it out to me. "Good."

"You said—"

"I know. This is for fishing without a license. Sixty dollars. When I run somebody in for PND I hand-deliver'em. No ticket."

"But I've never fished in my life."

You drove your elbow into my stomach. "Be quiet, David."

"Kepler discovered that orbits were elliptical, right?"

"You're taking night classes. History of physical sciences."

"Does this look like a classroom?" He leaned toward you, shook his head. "Scandal is ugly, Miss. Ugly."

"Stop that," I shouted.

He ambled down the beach. "The third law had to do with the period of revolution."

Sheridan stretched northwest to Minnesota that night and we drove a couple of days before reaching my apartment. With the extra distance the moon had to travel, night slowed down enough that we were in bed by two. Still, you did not say much. We dragged our bodies like sacks of sand across the bedroom floor, the floorboards sagged and splintered beneath our massive feet, and when we collapsed upon the mattress, we sank so low that the polyfoam rose up between us like an earthen dam. High-speed emotion can weigh a body down, make seconds seem like weeks and the curved seem straight, but lying there in the darkness I discovered that nothing is so heavy as the silence surrounding a lover asleep. I was unconscious for several days that night. When I woke I felt the inertia of age in my legs and arms. It was nearly noon. You had already gone home.

Götter will be an eigenvalue or better, a conformal tensor, G^{oter}, and Parmel will be . . . Parmel will be a constant, K, and . . . and Bethge will be the coefficient of Dunn, BD (Big Deal!), and St. Germaine is a square; Henkel can be (perfect) the function of Percy (Percy comes as close to being an absolute value as they've got; should maybe make him the base; his symbol, BS, for Blue Skin but also . . .), h(BS), and what would be the logarithm of Schwarzenfaber? (Franklin just may be a vector, force and direction, but will he be there?)

"This is not the Inquisition, I assure you." Percy pauses, becomes so sober that his jaws turn indigo. "But several of us have questions, you know, about this . . . er . . . particle." He enunciates the word like a spinster extracting a frog from a street urchin's pocket. As if he fears it will soil the other words of the sentence: this . . . this . . . ugh . . . particle.

"Look here, David," Henkel leans forward, spits out, "you can't just say these things. There are more concerns here than simply your own."

Percy raises his hand; Henkel hisses, leans back.

"You forget, David, Georg's reputation is at stake." Franklin *is* here. There are some snickers. Henkel glares over at him.

"The *department*'s reputation is at stake, gentlemen." Percy's voice is like baking soda thrown on a fire. The smiles vanish.

St. Germaine frowns. "Can we get you something, David? An aspirin?"

A cube, I think, a quadratic equation.

"In your lecture, you discussed some notions which were, to say the least, radical." Percy folds his hands, rocks back.

"To say the least." Henkel.

"We thought you might like the opportunity to speak to us more, well . . . more intimately about them."

"We have some questions, of course," Parmel puts in, "but everyone here is prepared to let you have your say." He appears so earnest that his eyebrows seem in danger of slipping off his head.

Götter stares, says nothing. Schwarzenfaber is, I think, asleep.

"Come on, David, you'll never get so much silence from this crowd again." Everyone glares at Franklin.

Percy smiles bluely. "We're waiting, David."

I will say nothing. I will say nothing. I stand, take the large, perfectly round Washington State apple which I have been concealing in my coat pocket, hold it before them—it is familiar; they know its history—polish it upon my sleeve, walk over to Henkel, hold it over his head. Franklin grins. The others draw their brows.

"David, I think—" Percy begins, but I silence him with a look.

I hold the apple in the air, turning it slowly around—Henkel fidgets, tries not to glance upwards—then I let it go.

Everyone gasps.

It hovers there a moment, then gradually gains speed, rises toward the fluorescent light, pins itself against the ceiling.

"Gentlemen, you may examine my equations."

Okay, so we forget GM_E/r_E^2 and the constant, and General Relativity says acceleration is up and motion is relative to the position of the observer—the astronaut moving up sees the Earth falling away. All right. Then how do you explain the Twin Paradox? How come the brother on Earth grows older?

I read an article of yours in *General Rel and Gravitation* (1973 or 74), the one about the instantons. You're a bright guy, but you can't speak English.

If you don't want to get charged, don't break the law.

Nietzsche wrote, I am told, that laughter can uproot any truth, that nothing is so fixed that frivolity cannot spirit it away. And,

Katherine, I want to believe this. I still want to believe this. But standing at your screen door, today, with the words swarming like mites before my eyes, I felt unsure of so much. We smirked at gravitation, and felt light, but there was something earthen in our hearts. We fattened, gained weight, started down.

"But what if he does, David? It would be so... so seamy, so humiliating."

It was as if the clouds over the lake came in lower each day, shortening the expanse between sky and ground. At night flying home I felt you losing altitude, dropping behind. It was difficult, alone, to keep myself aloft. Sometimes I couldn't see you for the lights and trees.

"Our friends, our families, and, David, our jobs."

That was Dingle's objection. If from the astronaut's point of view the Earth is accelerating away from him, why doesn't time move at the same rate for both? But, you see, only one brother is the traveler, the other the stay-at-home. There is exertion associated with high-speed motion, altering courses, the resistance to what will draw you down, so that whenever you change position—even if you're traveling in a loop—time slows down, your weight is affected. The traveler will come home young.

There is something going on here a lot more fundamental than gravity. There was so much I hadn't experienced at the time I wrote the article. Take the particle people, Freedman, for instance. "Supergravity," and all that cosmic meta-housekeeping. They never answer the simplest question. Why don't the gravity waves flow together? Why doesn't universal attraction turn on itself? How come the gravitinos don't pile up into little black holes everywhere, sucking up electrons, caving in nuclei, pock-marking space like a sixteen-year-old's cheeks? Oh, they give you answers—well, this substantiality, you understand, is not quite exactly indivisibly unitary, I mean, y'know, nor unqualified by other equally potent cosmological forces, and consequently, speaking less anthropomorphically, etc., etc. Look, anything that complicated has got to be a rationalization.

Now listen, I enjoy a joke as much as the next person, but this indecency business is nothing to laugh about.

"I'm confident, Katherine."

"I'm worried."

"I'm a cop. And a cop isn't paid to make jokes. You break the law, you get charged."

"There is no law, and I don't think you're really a cop."

"Five nights a week I'm a cop, and nobody says you gotta believe in the law. You just gotta obey it."

"Where's your sense of humor?"

"Me? I've got a terrific sense of humor. A regular clown. But the guy who'll preside at your trial, now there's a sober son-of-a-bitch."

"It isn't worth it, David," you said hugging your leg and rocking back and forth on your apartment floor.

I placed my hand on your arm. "But the lake."

You shook your head. "It isn't worth it."

So that was the night we rode to the top of the Hancock Building, thinking maybe we could get above it, you know, but, standing before the glass, as you stared into the black sky, I could already feel you growing heavy, knew that your gravity was returning, and that the struggle was not between you and me anymore but between the two of us and something larger—force, physics, the Earth.

"It's my birthday tonight, David." You stared through the observation window, your pupils dilated as if they were fixed upon the whole of the water or the sky or on whatever lay behind them.

"Why didn't you tell me?" I slipped my hand inside your shirt, ran my finger along the butter-smooth paraboloid of your breast. "We'll have to celebrate."

You shook your head, stepped away. "Don't."

"We're alone; no one can see." I edged closer. "We'll find a different beach, somewhere up toward Evanston."

"I'm thirty-nine years old, David."

I reached out and touched the upward-spiraling ends of your hair. "I love you."

You put your face in your hands, began to cry. "I'm thirty-nine years old."

And suddenly I realized I would have to try what I must have already sensed would be futile, realized, as I stood there with your body so massive that it seemed impossible to move, that, if we were ever to fly again, this would have to be the moment.

I stepped toward you and without a word, pulling your full body to my chest, I leaned into the glass and together, with your hair warm against my throat and your sobs throbbing in my chest, we toppled out into space. It was a foggy night. The clouds were as transparent as radiation beyond the violet. I gazed down below us, saw the white lip of the lake snickering along the shoreline, felt the breeze smirking beneath my arms.

"Katherine," I whispered, "I don't understand. Open your eyes. The night is as black as any night, as all nights. Below us is a lake. I will call it—"

"Oh, stop it, David, stop it!"

And suddenly, we were falling.

"It isn't really your birthday, Katherine, or it's your twenty-fourth birthday, or only your eighteenth..."

The windows of the Hancock Building were becoming long black ribbons rushing past. Beneath us the street spread its curbs like a salivating maw.

"Each birthday is every birthday, and continually being born we grow—"

You broke free of my arms, walked toward the elevator. "I'll get a cab home."

"Wait, Katherine, I—"

"No," you said. The doors slid closed. "No."

If I try to tell them what I know, I will say too much. I always say too much when Katherine is not here. Sweat breaks out upon my cheeks. The apple is rancid. It slips from my hands, falls, strikes Henkel on the shoulder. Pulp and juice run down his lapel.

Henkel jumps up from his chair. "You bastard! You lousy bastard!"

"David, what is the meaning—"

Franklin has my arm. "Sit down, David," he says softly. "Sit down."

"You stupid, stupid bastard!"

Katherine is not here.

These black men with their folded newspapers, napkins, soggy cigars are, in truth, only one man. He is hired by the transit authority, a retired insurance salesman, and rides two, perhaps three hundred trains a day, always gets a seat—even during rush hour. He returns home at night just long enough to bathe, slip into the monogrammed pajamas given him by his daughter, the biochemist, and smoke the saliva-logged cigar which, impossibly, he manages to light. He unfolds his newspaper, reads it by his bedroom lamp. His bureau drawers are filled with freshly starched napkins.

Half a block east I can see the treetops of Washington Park. After Garfield come Fifty-eighth, Sixty-first, King Drive, Cottage Grove, and University. We pass a burnt-out apartment, some tumbling shotgun houses. For the most part, the homes are nicer here, with lots and trees. The lake is several blocks away and I wonder if its hazy shorelessness against the horizon is all of infinity some of these people will ever know.

The black man leans toward me, stares out the windows on my side of the train, dips his head as if he were trying to see beneath a roof. The intercom rasps out a stop, the train begins to slow. He sits very straight in his seat, wipes his lips once. His hand trembles slightly; he does not move.

In wonder, Aristotle said, philosophy is born, and on his notebook Newton wrote that he was *amicus Aristoteles* and Plato, too, though truth's friend more, but I am suspicious of this cultivated obfuscation in the presence of the too-readily known.

There is something frightful about simplicity. In Sèvres, France, is a platinum-iridium cylinder, the International Prototype Kilogram, by which all scales are measured, and the International Time Bureau in Paris monitors the 9,192,631,770 vibrations emitted by caesium-133 in the eighty most accurate clocks extant. But this afternoon I must seek comfort in the world Einstein made strange. I believe in the attractive force between all bodies, a force which grows stronger with close contact though not requiring it, but unlike Newton, I believe it can lift us from the ground. I believe an orbit is the straightest thing possible in curved space, and that though seeming to depart, matter, people, time, return endlessly. I believe that the shortest distance between two points is often a spiral and that in all frivolousness there is something high. I do not know if I will ever see you again, Katherine.

"...a new force for us, a new concept of universal attraction and the curvature of bodies, of rising risibility, human levitation, of equations which delight not just illumine, which shed weight as well as photons and, making light of darkness, enlighten, an age when theories are ethereal, when science, discovering acts of nature, will not uncover them, but, content to embellish with a brocade of functions, will flirt with definition, arouse but not possess, and, by turning from the technic mirror which pimps the world, will by strokes of genius keep our body of knowledge warm, when scientists, though cranks, are never bores, provide no planks for the houses of others, and so raising our own roof, erect science again, its root firmly sunk in the knowing we cannot understand, its upward thrust as high as thought can go, and thus growing youthful, as time flies, so will we, ascending radiation's curve, unwarping space, coming together while spreading apart, until scientia, courted by a wit as sprightly as muons and quarks, will, in returning to Earth, be set free, begin to float, and arrayed in the loveliness of numbers, will rise, will rise."

"Gentlemen, I present to you the force of levity."

Just over the edge of the podium I could see the backs of the first seats, their covering rough and dull green, and behind them a perfect line of their clones stretching backwards into the shadows at the rear of the hall. Empty. The exit lights shown. Beneath them, the doors had stopped swinging. I could hear nothing. In my throat the warmth of the podium light glowed.

Levity. I tapped the podium with my knuckle, softly, then harder. Two slow taps, three quick, hard ones, then two more. Tap, tap, TA-TA-TAP, tap . . . tap. The sound flowed away from me like vibrations in water, shoreward then back, each wave dissipated by returning ripples, until the tapping and its echo so muddled together that, soughing and spent, the sound lost itself in the general agitation of the air—sound's death. The silence felt cool in my ears. I looked about me for my briefcase.

"Hah! Hah! like you hit'em in the face with a bucketful of manure!"

I stopped, shaded my eyes, squinted into the darkness at the rear of the hall. I was alone. No one had been rude. All along I had known they wouldn't listen. No surprises. I heard a seat-back creak, the scratching of heavy soles on the floor. I was alone.

"What's the refractive index of ice?"

He was moving across the row of seats, starting down the aisle. "The lecture is over," I called out. "Everyone has gone." I waved my arms. "Over."

"But the best, the best was that part 'when a man falls in love . . .' Heeeee!" He passed the first tier, down into the light. The fat man's way of ambling toward me, thick hair, jowly. "If you could've been sitting where I was sitting." The golden mustache.

"What business have you got—"

"Listen, I would've paid money, paid money." He put a hand onto the apron and vaulted up onto the stage. "You know, it's nearly freezing on that lake tonight; water's like ice. Could turn a goose blue."

I took my briefcase from a chair behind me, began gathering my papers. "I really don't have patience for you right now."

"Hey! Where's your sense of humor?"

"How did you get here?"

"I got a question about your last note."

I glanced at my watch. "I have a train to catch."

"Look, it's possible, isn't it? Those levitons. You weren't joking."

"Joking? Of course, I was joking. I'm joking right now."

"But like that Feinberg did with the faster-than-photons, or the anti-matter guy..."

"Dirac."

"Yeah. Like that would explain why the universe is getting bigger, and Dicke's theory—"

"You're not a policeman."

He flashed a faceful of cuspids. "You paid the tickets, didn't you?"

I stared at him a moment.

He said nothing.

"Sure. It's possible." I shrugged, snapped my briefcase. "Definitely possible. I mean, General Relativity is just a balancing act. The speed of light is absolute, so everything else can slide—time, energy, space, gravity, etc. But science was still pretty dependent on sense perception then. Nothing faster than the eye, so light is basic. But if Feinberg is right about tachyons...After all, they thought positrons were pretty spooky, too, at first. Why not an inverted graviton? How come—" I turned toward the empty seats. "I don't know what's possible."

"Hey, maybe you and me could grab a drink someplace."

I held up my watch. "Train."

"Oh yeah. Sure, sure."

We didn't move.

"My friend. She thought..." The warmth from the podium light still hung in my throat. "She thought you'd really charge us."

He grinned. "I would have charged you. The law."

I regarded him a moment. The eyes had a blueness I'd never noticed at night. The mustache jumped. "Yeah." I picked up my briefcase. "Yeah."

His face was doing something strange.

"Well, see you around," I said.

Behind me I heard a muffled half-reply, almost a cough. I kept walking. Nothing. I looked back over my shoulder. His jowls seemed too high, and his cheeks tightly creased. The mustache hopped furiously.

"Something the matter?" I took a step back.

"I... I'm sorry," he choked out.

I came closer. "Something in your throat?"

Suddenly, he exploded. "The clothes!"

I stared at him. He was positively laughing. "Here now..."

He pointed, held his sides. His mouth worked helplessly. "Clo ...clo...clo..."

I lifted my coat skirts, gazed down my trouser leg. I was neat enough, white shirt, beige tie. My inseam was a little wrinkled, but... "All right, I've had enough of this foolishness from — "

"I've never..." he gasped, his arm pressed to his stomach. He bent forward. "I've never seen you..." He struggled for breath, then burst out, "...in CLOTHES!"

Katherine, there is in all things a swinging and a rhythm, a playfulness in space, and even cosmologists must work, love and sleep. I know that some people are leery of thinking, and often I, too, grow cold, but truth matters above all things, and the following propositions are certain. Heaviness of heart holds us to the Earth. With time, some people grow young. What you said in your note today was wrong:

> David, everything that goes up, EVERYTHING,
> must sooner or later fall down.

For watching his mustache hop about his nose, his blue eyes tearing, I began to feel the warmth slide down my throat, warmth like your hair, feel it spread into my chest and limbs, heating up my dry hams, swelling my lungs like steamy sacks of air. I began to grow dizzy. My heart thumped loud. And all at once, the floor collapsed, my shoes hovered in the air, and, Katherine, I was laughing.

"How do I look?" I wheezed, my arms wrapped about my belly, my torso rocking forth and back.

"Awful!" he howled, slapping his knee. "Awful!"

I flew home that night, my briefcase in my hand, my overcoat buttoned all the way to my chin, flew over the loop, circled the Sears and Wrigley buildings, hovered briefly beside the balconies

of Marina Towers, swung low along the river and let the cold air
fill my pants legs like balloons. I even floated for a time above the
lake, its water as black as in summer, and sniffed into my nostrils
the dampness of fog, then, swinging westward above the trees of
Lincoln Park, and, with my heart as light as a body in free fall, I
crossed Lake Shore Drive, aligned myself with the lights of Sheridan, and started home. There are certain kinds of knowing which
when spoken of seem over-proud and when heard necessarily
confuse. Huss was thought an humble man when silent, but
knew, as Newton proved, that any thought sealed up too tightly
will mortify, that silence is grave and leads there. So this afternoon I'll try again, will harangue and declare, "Now listen,
Percy, you old fart!" Will remain quiet only for politeness, will
damn their muddy eyes and make them feel the force that lets the
gravitinos frolic, sets the wind loose over water. I will be clever,
speak much too loudly, laugh as often as I can.

"UNIVERSITY STATION, HYDE PARK, MUSEUM OF
SCIENCE AND INDUSTRY." The intercom squawks like a por-
poise with a headcold.

I pull myself to my feet as the train slows down. The black man
also stands, starts to pocket his napkin, then thinks better of it,
bends, peers outside. I wait a moment for him to start toward the
door, then, when he doesn't move, slide around him. The train
jolts to a stop. The doors slide open. The sulphurous, sweet smell
of scalded air rushes up my nose, of electrons set free and the gas
emitted by the live rail. I step forward; a hand catches my shoulder.

"Excuse me, sir." I am looking into a black trench of flesh
swooping down from a tear duct, passing under one tumid nostril
to surround and raise up the mouth like a retaining wall. The skin
of the man's face is shiny, thick like the hide of a water animal.

I step back. "Yes?"

A fat child shoves past me. "Yer in the way!"

"Do you know the name of this train?" The man gazes momentarily into my face, then allows his spine to sag back against a
post. His eyes are yellow, wet.

"Where is it you want to go?"

The intercom blathers incoherently. He leans forward, points behind us. "I thought, back there..." Then gives a weary laugh, shakes his head. "I seem to be confused."

The pitch of the engine begins to rise. He lifts his hand to his mouth, coughs. I watch him a moment.

"One more stop and it starts back." I make a circular motion with my finger, smile. "Travels in a loop. All day."

He brightens. "That's good." Nods. "That's good."

"Yes."

He eases back down into his seat. I step onto the platform just as the doors slide closed. He is watching me. I smile—confidently, I hope. It is a dry fall afternoon. The walk to the school will be pleasant. The train lurches forward. It is hard to see through the windows. But I think he waves.

A Circle
is the Shape
of Perfection

On the morning of his thirtieth birthday Harry Sneltzer woke to the disquieting realization that he was becoming his father. He slid from his bed, stumbled into the bathroom and, staring at his sleep-glazed eyes in the mirror, tried out a few characteristic phrases: "Harry, son..." "Seen the paper?" "Can't find my socks." Yes, though a decade had passed since his father's death, Harry still remembered the voice well enough to recognize it— the rapid spitting out of syllables, an affinity for rising inflections, the explosive reiterations. Even his body this morning was not his own. He stared at his legs. Spindly and faintly bowed, with flesh too pale and hair too black and wiry, these were the legs Harry had seen beneath his father's heavy white-shirted torso in the hall of his parents' home. But worse than these physical transformations was a feeling—he had no idea from where it came—that at any moment he might say or do something that wasn't his own, that even his thoughts were coming from somewhere else. Was this a crisis, he wondered stepping into the shower? He fiddled with the water flow. He couldn't remember if his father had preferred warm or stinging cold.

"Harry, Son, it's good—GOOD—to see you again!"
Harry turned away from his office window and gazed into the

white incisors and bulbous jowls beaming at him from his desk.
"Dad. Why, what are you doing here?"

"Hah! That's good, Harry. That's clever. A real sense of
humor, that boy. What am *I* doing in *your* office? Is that it? Hah,
hah! Rich."

"Hah, hah..."

"But I've seen you looking better." His father frowned down
momentarily at Harry's briefcase resting on the floor to the side of
the desk, then cut his eyes at Harry thoughtfully. "Yes. I've
definitely seen you looking less peakish."

"Well, jeez, Dad, I guess it's this influence business."

"Influence?"

"Don't get me wrong. I liked you. It's just that... well, one of
you seemed enough."

His father came out from behind the desk and threw his arm
over Harry's shoulders. "Son, Son, life is fat with changes, swollen to bursting with them. You never know a minute you're not
being transformed, and today—TODAY—Harry, is just a small
kink in the customary order of things. Think of it this way: for the
first time in your life, you know before you finish where you will
conclude. That, Harry, is a privilege. Relax." He yanked the
briefcase from the floor and replaced it in the corner by the coat
tree.

"I don't like it."

"Now, Harry, you're acting a bit of the spoiled sport, don't you
think?"

"But I don't want to be you, Dad. I want to be me."

"Mee, schmee. Just do what you want, Son. It's that simple."

"But what I want is what you want."

"Wanted."

"Wanted."

"Hmmmm." Harry's father placed his own briefcase in the
space beside the desk and with a sigh lowered himself back into the
chair. "Then, Harry boy, looks like you've got a problem."

Harry finished his shower, dressed and caught the number ninety-two bus down to his office. He pushed open the door—same old unoiled whine—and stood gazing in. Perhaps the office was part of his difficulty. They had moved him only a couple of weeks ago, on the day after he'd received his bank statement. He could remember the day clearly because the statement wasn't just the monthly; it was the bi-annual—the one with his savings, too. And this statement was more significant than others. A fifth digit had at last materialized to the left of the decimal. Ten thousand thirty-six dollars and odd cents. But instead of drawing his usual confidence from these numbers, Harry had felt depressed. He could go back to school now if he wanted, take a leave of absence, travel, even pick up his saxophone again. Still there was something unresolved about these new possibilities, something threatening. He had eaten too much for supper that night and gone to bed with a stomachache.

Then the next morning when he had arrived at his office the furniture was missing.

"We're moving you, Harry," Callen had said, his eyes half open and a smile drooping across his chin. "Need the space for the girls. You'll be in with Requisitions. Fifth floor."

Harry had stared back at him. "Fifth floor? That's my father's old—"

Callen had nodded sleepily. "Yeah. The super remembers. Says it's even the same office."

And though there was no way to be sure if the supervisor had known what he was talking about or not, enough of the details were right to make Harry wonder—the perpetually swinging brass light fixture, the crack in the plaster by the door, the top window pane whited-out then scratched partially clear again. He walked over to his desk and lowered himself into the chair. Its casters rolled smoothly with only the faintest squeak. Honey-colored with a badly scored seat and sweat-darkened arms, it clearly had a couple of decades' use behind it and might have been Harry Sr.'s own. Harry felt a cold prickling in his shoulders as he leaned back. The springs sang softly. He lifted his heels into a shallow worn depression above the left desk drawers. They fit perfectly.

The phone was ringing:

"Sneltzer, Purchasing."

"Is this Harry?"

"Yes."

"Harry Sneltzer?"

"Yes."

"Hal, it's Frog!"

Frog?

"Go and ask the Devil, hey! He remembers too, hey! Nobody can forget the class of '42, hey-hey!"

Silence.

"You sound great, Hal. Haven't changed a bit."

"Excuse me, but I believe—"

"Listen, I'm only here until the afternoon. What say we grab a bite? Lots to tell. Lots."

"Sir..."

" 'Sir'?"

"I believe you want my father."

Silence.

"Hal?"

"Well, 'Harry' really. My father and I—"

"This Harry Sneltzer?"

"Well, technically, I suppose—"

"Listen, Hal, I'd know your voice anywhere. It's great you know, just to...well...it's been a hell of a long time. How's the old girl? What's her name?"

"Minette is my mother's—"

"Minette, Minette, Minette. Wow, how you forget something like that. Hey listen, Hal, I've got to go but—"

"Excuse me, but I'd better explain."

"No time now, Hal, save it. How about you meet me at the Sheraton, say one-ish?"

''Just a minute.''

''Hey, Hal, do you remember the time you and me and . . . and . . . and Annette, yeah, down at . . . oh hell, where was it? You know, the beach place.''

''You've got the wrong person!''

''No, Hal, I remember. It was you all right because we were driving your old Ford.''

''No, I mean—''

''Well, gotta run. At the Sheraton, little after one.''

''No, I can't—''

''Looking forward to it Harry.''

''But—''

''Skidoo.''

Skidoo?

Harry took his briefcase from his lap, placed it on the floor to the side of his desk, stood, paced across the room and back. He would be reasonable, he decided. There was no danger of actually becoming his father, not with any precision anyway. Genetics was unavoidable, and a certain amount of similarity, environmental influences, even an occasional—what would you call it—lapse of personality, repetition of paternal behavior. These things had to be taken into account. Still, similarity, repetition, lapses were not metamorphosis. He was familiar with this matter of fathers and sons and knew he was within a context. Strange things had occurred here, but still there were laws, patterns, cycles. He wondered if he should draw comfort from such facts. He was not sure.

On the morning of his thirtieth birthday Harry Sneltzer turned over, clicked off the alarm, went back to sleep.

A knock on his office door:

''Harry, it's your mother.''

Harry got up, opened the door. "Mom, really nice of you to come—"

"I won't be any bother, Harry. Just dropped by to wish you happy birthday." She strode four steps into the office and stopped. She had on a white dress Harry hadn't seen before, had her hair pulled high up onto her head, her neck bare. "So strange to be here again. Nothing has changed. Nothing."

"Then this *is* Dad's old office?"

She smiled. "How could I forget? Number 413. I used to come here every day. I'd bring the sandwiches. He'd have the coffee."

The dress made him uncomfortable. It was of a coarsely woven, lightweight fabric, the kind the wind caught easily. "Mom?"

"I'd sit right here, and he'd sit there where you're sitting."

"Mom, this is 418. To the right off the elevator, then two lefts. Not 413."

She stopped, drew her brows down low over her eyes. "I wouldn't forget something like that."

Harry stared out his office window. He knew that there were certain clear differences between himself and his dad. By Harry's age his father was married, had a kid (Harry, Jr.), a house, a bad pulse. And he had been balder. Though that might have been later. Harry recalled the wisps of hair clogging the comb lying on his own bathroom sink. Well, other differences then.

Harry padded back across the tile floor to the door he had left standing open. He flipped it closed with a deft backhand movement and returned to his desk. Now there was something of his own. Small perhaps, but no one else closed a door like that.

Harry smiled, slid a purchase order out of his "in" box and began to fill in the blanks. Of course, he knew you couldn't be certain about origins. It was possible, just possible, that even this gesture was an inheritance, something he might have picked up somewhere. Still no use tracing patterns in smoke.

Harry leaned back, gazed at the partially completed order form in front of him. His handwriting looked strange today, different somehow. Maybe he just hadn't noticed it in awhile. The letters were shorter, lower, with less hump than he remembered, a kind of general flattening into indecipherability. He shifted in his chair. How often had his mother complained that his dad's *u*'s and double *e*'s were indistinguishable, and his *e*'s and *l*'s, and his *m*'s and *w*'s?

Do something, Harry thought. Something clearly and unmistakably different. He got up from his desk, started out of the office.

"Don't mean to be rude now, Dad, but ... er ... that's not your desk anymore. Remember?"

"Hah, hah!" His father plucked a wad of purchase order forms from a drawer and with a sweep of his arm cleared a work area on top of the desk.

"What is a father anyway, Harry?"

Harry tried to slip his leg casually between his father's knee and the desk drawer, but the knee wouldn't budge. "Er ... Dad, maybe if you could just slip back a little ... let me in here to my desk a minute."

"After all, the father isn't a person. That's a common mistake." Harry's father pulled a folder from the file drawer, stared at it blankly for a moment, then dropped the contents into the waste-basket.

"Dad! That's my correspondence."

"I mean, let's be mature, Harry. Let's be sensible. We understand biology, reproduction, chromosomes, not to mention your logic, your 'if A does not equal B, then B does not, cannot equal A.' Use your common sense. You're you. I'm me. You can't *really* become me."

Harry put his hands on the back of his father's chair, began to tug. His father hooked his fingers under the drawer ledge.

Harry gritted his teeth. "I wish I could be sure of that."

SOMETHING CLEARLY ...

Harry Sneltzer caught a cab across town to the Fifth Street

Bridge. He asked the driver to stop on the bridge. The cabbie eyed him nervously. Harry dug into his pockets and took out his roll of bills, Diner's card, some change. The cabby took it slowly, did not smile. Harry stepped out of the car, walked toward the edge, climbed over the railing. The sun came up hot and bright from the water. From somewhere he heard voices. The wind slapped at his face.

SOMETHING CLEARLY AND UNMISTAKABLY...
Harry Sneltzer purchased a dress, no ordinary dress, this one, but a Dior shirtwaist with pleated skirt. To the tune of three bills. There was some difficulty. He wanted a very large size. The saleswoman eyed him suspiciously. He asked to try it on.

SOMETHING CLEARLY AND UNMISTAKABLY DIFFERENT.
Harry Sneltzer hopped a freight train to Tucson...or Three Flats, Nevada...or Montreal or...or...

Harry sat in a rust-pitted diner two blocks and down a service alley from his office. He had never eaten here before. Clearly and unmistakably it was not his father's sort of place.

"So, Heery, have you been thinking about my offer?"

A coincidence of place, timing. Donald Sowerby, longtime business associate and friend of Harry's father, had seen him on the street, walked with him to this diner, was seated in the other half of Harry's booth.

Harry regarded the apple that Don had taken from his coat pocket and placed on the table. "Well, I'm always thinking, Don."

"You know, me being your dad's buddy and all, and him being gone...well, seems if I got a good thing, I should pass it on. You know what I mean?" Don had his own management firm now and at intervals offered Harry various positions there.

"Sure."

"And I know it's . . . well . . . not the main consideration, but . . . Lotsa bucks, Heery."

Forty-three thousand thirty-six dollars and odd cents. Harry nodded at the apple. "Breakfast?"

"Diet."

Harry considered the possibility of confiding in Don—another perspective might be helpful, especially from an old friend of his father's—but immediately recognized the difficulties. How would you begin? Uh . . . Don, these legs remind you of anyone? How about the way I shut this door? Or even worse: Don, I have a problem. Seems I am my dad, or in a few days will be, and. . . . Harry took a sip of his coffee. "It's my birthday."

Don brightened, extended his hand. "Then congratulations, huh?"

"My thirtieth."

Don became sober; his eyebrows slid over the edges of his forehead. "Yeah, thirty and sixty. Those are the tough ones. You know, Heery, I'm fifty-seven myself."

Harry nodded gravely. His father would have been fifty-nine.

"I remember when I turned thirty. Nearly put me under. I didn't want to go home to the wife, didn't want to see my kids, wanted to quit, run away. Then in a week or so, like nothing ever happened."

"Yeah."

"But your dad, now . . ."

Harry's head came up.

"A funny guy, Heery. I mean him and me were real close, but he was . . . well, he didn't show a lot of things." Don took a bite of the apple, worked it meditatively over into his cheek.

"I remember thinking that it wasn't much to him—growing older. He came to the office, a nice word for the girls out front, everything like usual."

Don paused, shook his head. "But like I say, a funny guy. It was a few weeks later. I'd thought everything was past. We were at this joint down the way having some beers, when out of the clear blue, he's looking somewhere way off, and he says, 'I'm dying, Don.' Well, I looked him up once and say, 'What do you mean? You seen a doctor?' But he shakes his head, as if to say, 'No, no, you got it all wrong,' and then he looks at me with his eyes squinched like this, see, and his mouth tight and his hands just hanging there limp and relaxed and says it again. 'I'm dying.' Then he looks back down at his drink, and that's all he'd say."

Harry regarded Don silently. "Maybe you're right, Don. Maybe a change is what I need."

"We'd like to have you, Heery."

"I'll let you know."

Harry continued to watch the steam rising from his coffee, then stood. There was a twinge in his back. Sitting too long. Or an old injury. "Guess I'd better be getting back."

Don lifted the remainder of the apple in farewell. "And, Heery, happy birthday, huh?"

On the morning of his thirtieth birthday Harry Sneltzer woke to the startling realization that everything was possible, that he was no one at all. Therefore anyone. He sprang from bed, stalked to his window, threw it open. Air, air. From here he could see for miles. Steeples, small homes, the city not far away, a park, a tennis court in someone's back yard. Nothing blocked his view.

"Sorry to have to come to this, Dad, but a man's desk . . . well, his desk is like his soul." Harry slipped his arm in a headlock around his father's chin. "Sometimes you have to fight for it."

His father gave an urbane chuckle and sunk his teeth into Harry's biceps.

"YEOW!" Harry stumbled backwards.

"Nope, Harry. The father's not a person. He's a name, a label, a catchall. Certain things happen, see, and we call 'em 'Dad.' " His father swiveled his chair around to face Harry.

Harry began to approach with his back bent and hands out as he had seen wrestlers do. "What things?" He lunged for his father's arm. A kick from the blind side spun him to the floor.

"Some mutt pees on your wingtips or your wife's calves turn to grapevines or you get a chink in your fender." Harry's father leaned forward. "You all right?"

Harry moved slowly along the sidewalk back toward his office. He knew genetics, occasional lapses, repetition couldn't account for everything. There were persons. They made decisions. Took control. Opened their own way. Still, repetition could turn your head. It might not prove anything, but it brought you up, made you wonder.

He gazed down at the sidewalk. He wished that the spaces between the cracks were less regular, or that the cracks were broken somehow, stood at angles. It was as if you were walking in one of those exercise hoops for pet rodents. Whop, whop, whop. The cracks kept coming up. Or maybe it was the same crack. Harry turned around, stared back at the squares of sidewalk behind him. No, he wasn't standing still.

He turned, did a quick dance step around the next crack, jogged once left, once right, past the next two, took a short hop over the fourth, then started walking again. His left foot struck every other one.

"I don't understand it, Harry," his mother sighed. "It's not right, getting old, forgetting important things. This seems so much like the same office."

Harry gazed back at her nervously. Though he was certain he had never seen the dress before, it seemed strangely familiar—as if it already had a place in his memory. Maybe he had seen someone in the office wearing one. "You're . . . you're not old yet, Mom."

She waved him off. "I know how old. Maybe they changed the numbers or something."

"I suppose it's possible."

"Well, I won't bother you, Harry. I know you have work."

"There's no hur—"

"I can't sit around all day either, you know. Come. Let me give you a kiss. Your birthday."

Harry leaned forward. He became conscious of an old smell, not powder or perfume, something in her hair or on her hands or mouth. He heard the distant screech of seabirds. Her lips touched his lightly. They were damp.

"Happy birthday, Harry."

Seabirds?

Again, the phone:

"Sneltzer, Purchasing."

"Hal, hey, where are you?"

Silence.

"I mean, I been waiting now half an hour."

"Excuse me, sir, but there's been a mistake."

"Huh?"

"This is not Hal Sneltzer. I mean, it is...but it's not the Hal Sneltzer—"

"Hey, look Hal, I haven't got a lot of time."

"I'm not Hal Sneltzer!"

"But you said—"

"You want my father."

"Your father!"

"This is Harry Sneltzer, Jr."

"Your father!"

"Yes, we have the same names and our voices...uh...I am told, are similar, but the man you want...that is, I am his son."

"Well, God bless me. I knew you when, well, I knew you before you...Well, listen son, get your dad for me, huh? Tell him its Frog. Say to him—now get this—say:

"Go and ask the Devil, hey! He remembers too, hey—"

"He's dead."

"No one forgets the class— What's that?"

"The man you want—my father—he's dead."

Pause. "Hal?"

"No."

"This Harry Sneltzer?"

Silence.

"You know, Hal, you sound great. Haven't changed a bit."

"I said, No!"

"Hey, Hal, listen. I've got a plane to catch in —"

"I am not Hal Sneltzer!"

"I know it's kind of spur of the moment, but after all, thirty years nearly..."

Harry hung up.

When Harry got back to his office, he took a yellow legal pad from a desk drawer and wrote in large letters at the top of the page: WAYS TO BE DIFFERENT FROM YOUR FATHER. Along the left margin he numbered one to twenty-five. He studied this, then wrote "Be evil" beside number one, "Be adventurous" by number two, hesitated at three, then after a moment added, "Be extreme." He started to strike out number three, wondering if it weren't included in the first two but decided to let it stay. After all, evil wasn't always extreme. You could be moderately evil. Same thing for adventurous. For number four he wrote, "Buy a plaid suit," then crossed it out.

Harry didn't have any other ideas so he went back to number one. "Be evil." He gazed down for a long minute at the yellow pad. Maybe being evil was central. God was a father, wasn't he? But then there was original sin, and who was responsible for that? Harry began to get confused, so he straightened his coat and strode out of the office.

When Harry returned, he was smiling and held his coat tightly closed across his chest. His pockets rattled as he walked. The Requisition clerk had been on break, and slipping into the supply closet while Diane, his secretary, wasn't looking had been a cinch. Harry pulled two boxes of green Lindy pens from inside his coat and laid them on the desk, then a bag of paper clips, two jumbo gum erasers, a Rolodex refill and an ink pad from his right flap pocket, a typing ribbon cartridge from each of his hip pockets, a linear-metric conversion ruler from under his belt and from his

left flap pocket—his one bit of rashness—a chrome-plated
Swingline 3000 stapler, fresh from the box. He arranged these in
ascending order—paper clips to stapler—across his desk and lowered himself into his chair. In the setting of his office the objects
seemed disappointingly familiar. He concentrated on the stapler
for some seconds then began poking at the boxes with his finger.
Despite the originality of his theft, it still rested on the surface of
things.

He cleared his throat. "Harry, son..." "Seen the paper?"
"Can't find..." No, no. He sighed, reached for the yellow tablet.
Try something else.

Harry shook his head to clear it, rolled onto his side. His shoulder ached where it had hit the floor. "But I'm not worried about
my wingtips, Dad. I'm worried about you." He noticed that the
feet of the desk chair were little more than an arm's length away
and calculated that, if he moved quickly enough, he might be able
to slip a hand under the chair and tip it. He maneuvered for
position.

"Worried? Son, Son, who isn't worried? You think I'm not—
wasn't—worried? Look at me. I step out of my office and when I
come back, I don't know the place. We're dealing with forces here,
Harry, not persons."

With a kick Harry propelled his body forward and thrust out his
arms. His hands touched the cold brass of the casters. "Then you
don't think my problem is really with you?" He felt his father's
fingers clutching at his hair and ears, but the old man was too
slow. Harry yanked. His father's legs shot up, and head and
flailing arms struck the floor with a thud.

"Er...ah...good move, Son."

"Be evil." "Be adventurous." Harry lowered the yellow tablet
onto the desk and pushed the stapler, pens, ruler, erasers, clips,
cartridges, pads and Rolodex refill into a pile at one side. Surely,

something different had to be possible. He glanced back at the tablet. "Be extreme." But extremity didn't seem to exist, or rather seemed to exist both as itself and its opposite. As is and is not. As father and son. Harry gazed down at the floor, noticed the band of white flesh above the tops of his socks. He lifted his cuffs for a better look.

Too old, he thought frowning. Too old.

On the morning of his thirtieth birthday Harry Sneltzer was still sitting up in bed, eyes bleary but wide open, hands twisting the sheet in his lap. The clock ticked loudly in his ear. He had not slept all night.

"You know, Harry, sometimes when you stand there like that..." She hesitated, one hand resting on the knob of the half-open door, then laughed. "Oh, just listen to the old woman."

Harry's face felt hot. Maybe the birds had flown over from the river. He had seen gulls perched on the awnings before. But that smell.... "This may sound unusual, Mom, but have you ever... I mean, before something happened to you, did you ever remember it?"

"Memory can do funny things."

"But even in advance? Before it's a memory?"

"Like your father and me, for instance. Even now, after ten years, I still have trouble believing... You know, it would still seem so natural just to come here, to this office."

The ocean! That was it. Salt air. But how— "Mom, you haven't been to the beach, have you?"

She looked startled. "The beach?"

"I know it's crazy, but there's this smell, in your hair, like the ocean."

"The... the beach..."

Harry looked down at her. A wisp of hair had come loose, hovered lightly above her ear.

"Don't tease an old woman, Harry."

The wind lifted her skirt. It billowed cloudlike and settled again about her knees.

"I'm not teasing."

"It would seem so natural. After all these years. He'd stand there where you are standing."

Harry reached past her, closed the door with a click. "You know, you don't have to go, Mom."

"You have work to do."

He took her hand, helped her from the car. "It can wait."

"What if someone comes?" She stepped closer.

He placed his arm about her waist. He could hear the hiss of the water gliding over the sand. His fingers felt her skin beneath the thin fabric. "It's been a long time."

"Oh, Harry, Harry..."

"Minette."

Phone number, phone number. Got to find. Harry plowed through matchbooks, paper scraps, pieces of kleenex in his desk drawer.

Ah hah.

He held up a crumpled business card, reached for the telephone.

6...

Don? This is Harry Sneltzer... Yeah. Got a couple of questions about that job... Nothing serious, you know—

...3...

But I've been thinking, and... well, I'd like to discuss it with you. No decision yet.

...4...

Don? Harry here... You free tomorrow for lunch? Yeah. You may be right, Don. A guy reaches a certain age and, well, maybe we can—

...2...

Don? Harry... yeah, old Harry. I think I'll take it. Just decided. A fresh start, Don. Offices side by side again. New faces—

...9...

Don? Me. Look, let's do it. It's dead here, and no sense me beating a corpse...Yeah, like old times. Oh, Minette sends her best. And the kid—

...0...

No decision yet. No decision yet. Just, just—

Harry inserted his finger in the dial, turned once more, held. He would let go; it would spin back; there would be a pause, some clicking, a ring.

...2...

Don? This is old Harry Hal Sneltzer new me Jr. Sr. old times like something fresh offices—

He slammed the receiver down.

Harry stared down into his father's face. He was perched on the old man's chest, one hand pinning a limp wrist to the floor, the fingers of the other wrapped around his father's throat. His father's breathing was short, choked.

"Okay, okay, Harry. You win. You've got me. Now finish it. Kill me off."

"Kill you?" His father's throat was much smaller than Harry had remembered, softer with almost no whiskers or razor burns. He felt the adam's apple rolling like a marble beneath his thumb.

"Don't get me wrong. It's not fair. Not for a minute is it fair. Snotty-nosed kid like you comes sauntering in here, doesn't know purchase orders from play-dough, kicks the old man in the ass, gets away with it every time. But no use crying for justice. There's no justice."

"All I wanted was my desk—"

"Oh, come off it." With the index finger of his free hand, Harry's father jabbed Harry in the chest. "Your mother, Harry, was a beautiful woman. A BEAUTIFUL woman."

"I...I'm sure she was attractive, Dad, but—"

"BEAUTIFUL!"

"All right, but what's that go to do—"

"Oh yeah. Right. That's got nothing to do with it. Nothing."

"Dad, I'm turning into my father! I'm becoming you!"

"You think you got problems? You wouldn't know problems if they ran over you." He leaned forward. "I'm dead, Harry. Dead."

Harry rocked back onto his heels. "I'm sorry." He stood, walked over to the window. "I forgot."

"But, no, no. You sons! You wouldn't know anything about that."

Harry stared out the window. "I turned thirty years old today."

"So kill me then."

Harry shrugged. "What's the good?"

"Oh, don't get morose, Harry. You're still young. Find yourself a girl. Forget about it."

"Young..."

"You're becoming me, but so what else is new? You've been becoming me a long time."

Harry could hear the casters rolling across the floor.

"But the office, my voice, the way I close doors..."

"You're alive, Harry. ALIVE!"

"And Mom, she...she was beautiful."

He heard the faint singing of springs.

"Yeah. Hah, hah! Beautiful."

Hah, Hah?

Harry spun around. Just in time. His desk chair rose up grim and massive before him, crashed into his face, carried him backward. The window exploded around him. Harry grabbed at the molding. Tried to hold himself in.

"Bastard!" he yelled.

His father chuckled and charged again. "We're all bastards, Harry."

On the morning, on the morning, on the morning...

The air is cool, cooler than any of them had expected. The old Ford coughs along over the sand. The smell of salt water fills

Harry's head. Minette is close to his side. Her breast brushes his elbow. By the door Frog is asleep.

"And he got us up at five o'clock," Harry laughs softly. " 'Don't want to miss sunrise on the beach.' "

Minette smiles but makes no reply. They both know they would rather be alone. There is a cloud bank over the water. The tide is low, quiet. The sun is up, and though its rising was in its way spectacular—streaks of fuchsia, ocher, and mauve—Harry feels oddly disappointed. As if there is no connection between a thing seen and its expectation.

After a time they stop. Frog mumbles something but does not wake. Harry helps Minette from the running board. She has on a white dress of a lightweight, coarsely woven fabric that the wind billows about her knees. They start down the beach. She takes his arm.

Somewhere out of sight of the car they stop walking. The morning is still cool, but they decide to put on their suits anyway. Minette steps behind a dune. Harry keeps watch.

Over the water large gray birds are flying. Harry has often wondered if there are names for all the different kinds of birds, and if so, who could possibly know them. He has wondered similar things about dictionaries and encyclopedias and all the different languages and insects. Once shortly after his fourteenth birthday he set out to read the entire Webster's from front to back. He read two and a half pages a day for three weeks. At the end of that time he pinched together the read pages and, staring at the edge of the book, compared them to the unread. He suddenly became very frightened. He ran outside and squatted between two tall shrubs in his parents' front yard, sat there staring up at the night sky. After awhile he came back inside but could not get to sleep.

Minette comes from behind the sand dune. Her suit shows her long legs, and Harry tries hard not to stare but seems unable to turn away. She colors slightly. For a few minutes they do not speak.

Harry would like to tell Minette something, something that neither of them will ever forget, that will make them both smile the fine, sober smile of people who understand things, but cannot think of a word that would begin. He knows that he wants to tell her he is strong, that the world will be difficult, of course, but finally will yield to them. He wants to tell her of the seven truths in the universe which do not change. He wishes he knew the name of these birds.

After a moment they hear Frog calling from down the beach. Minette turns to Harry and laughs. "Aren't you going to put on your suit?"

Harry nods, yep, yep, and stumbles off through the sand toward the dune.

"You know, Harry...sometimes when you stand there like that..." Harry's mother hesitated, one hand resting on the knob of the door, then laughed. "Silly, silly woman."

"It was nice of you to remember, Mom." Harry reached past her and held the door.

"Old people don't forget birthdays."

In the hall he saw Diane, the Requisitions secretary, walk past, the thin skirt of her white dress sailing behind her. Harry smiled. The dress! So that's where..."Come back any time."

"Oh, don't be so polite, Harry. I'm your mother."

Harry chuckled. He watched her swing past the doorjamb, heard her heels hit the tiles. Then silence. Harry peered into the hall. His mother was standing on tiptoe, staring up at something above the door. "I just wanted to check," she said. "In the light, you know." She nodded her head, pointed. "418."

A last time, the phone:

"Sneltzer, Purchasing."

"Hey Hal, how much longer you gonna be? I mean it's getting late."

"Late?"

"Yeah, I tried to tell you. I'm only here this afternoon, then it's on the big bird again. I mean they don't pad us old timers like they do the young ones, you know. They give us one day and that's all you can take."

"Late."

"Yeah, and Hal, after all these years. I mean, if I go back and don't see you . . . Hal, you know what it does to old Frog."

"Well, it's been a hell of a day."

"Oh, don't think I don't understand, Hal."

"And my birthday, too. It's my birthday."

"No kidding? Jeez. Things get popping so fast that birthdays kind of get lost in the shuffle."

"Yeah."

"And a fellow just doesn't have the pizzazz he once did, you know. Not that we're old yet, Hal, but . . . well, I know how it can get."

"Yeah, you know how it can get."

"Sure."

"Frog . . ."

"Yeah?"

"Really good to hear your voice, Frog."

"You too, Harry. I can't get over—"

"Hey, Frog, you remember that time, you and me and Minette, in the old Ford, at the beach . . ."

"Hal, I was just thinking of that today. Can you believe it? Just today."

"Yeah. How long's it been Frog?"

"Oh Hally, don't ask me that one. Who wants to count?"

"Listen. Where are you?"

"Well, I told you, Hal. The Sheraton. You were gonna meet me."

"Maybe I can get by now."

"Not much time left, Hal."

"Well, I'll try."

"Try hard, Hal."

"Frog?"

"Yeah."

"Your voice . . ."

"I know, Hal, I know."

"Skidoo."
"Skidoo."

Harry spent the remainder of the day sitting in his chair, a pen balanced between his fingers. In the afternoon he bought a sandwich from a vending machine then returned to his office and, after turning it over several times on top of his desk, dropped it unopened into a drawer. He didn't go out for his break. At five the clatter of shoes rose from the hall, but Harry didn't leave his chair. Shortly after seven the slit of light beneath his door went dark. Still he remained there. Finally, much later, he slid from his chair, picked up his briefcase and moved toward the door. In the evening dimness the room seemed very bare, no pictures, no drapes. A calendar hung on the wall to the left of the desk, and Harry could make out the shape of a large insect lumbering across its open page. What was different today from ten years before? Some cracks plastered; a few tiles replaced.
SOMETHING CLEARLY...
"What is a father anyway?"
...CLEARLY AND UNMISTAKABLY...
"Your mother, Harry, was a beautiful woman."
...CLEARLY AND UNMISTAKABLY DIFFERENT.
If only he knew the name of those birds.
Harry watched the insect a moment longer, then took a memo pad from his desk, stepped toward the calendar, raised the pad in his hand... but no. He turned, strode out the door and passed into the darkness of the hall.

On the morning of his thirtieth birthday Harry Sneltzer woke

NOVEMBER 14, 1864

1.

Old things make me nervous. New ones make me mad. I'm suspicious that the burnings were deliberate, that even Sherman was part of a plan. Didn't the 1917 fire start at City Hall? "And all this gibberish about rising from ashes," I want to exclaim in elevators, cafe booths, crowded halls. "Everybody knows the Phoenix did itself in."

Most evenings I stand here on this hill overlooking the ninth green of Atlanta's downtown park and stare out at the city as the golfers slouch home. A mile to the northwest, Colony Square squats like a day laborer eating beans and squints back at me from behind the condemned apartments of Piedmont Drive. Nearer, the flag atop the old Sears smirks lewdly around the press box of a high school football stadium, and to the south someone has rammed Peachtree Center Plaza into the sky. I come here because these images provide evidence for me. Clearly, we are trapped in a pernicious rise and fall. I come here to sing out: "These are processes!" But the golfers cannot hear me. And I come here to get away from Mrs. Bellamy.

"We are soldiers, Joseph, the last guard of a noble army, beaten but never vanquished, which the vulgar horde has driven from its land." Mrs. Bellamy speaks like this when seated in her den on her camelback divan. She pinches her ivory cigarette holder between an arthritic index and thumb, sucks smoke into her head and allows it to seep out her nostrils as she speaks. "Yankees, Joseph, are vulgar."

Though I do not share Mrs. Bellamy's opinions, I find the salary she pays me very persuasive and so raise few objections. "Would you like for me to tell you about Inman Park?"

"They are incapable of appreciating civilization."

"Euclid Avenue looks almost like it did in the nineties."

"That is why they burn things. Burn things and build projects."

"I don't believe there are any projects in Inman Park, Mrs. Bellamy."

"You must call me 'Aunty.' Everyone must call me 'Aunty.'"

If I close my eyes, swallow hard and think only of my malnourished checking account, even this can be done. "Yes... Aunty... Bellamy."

Mrs. Bellamy does not know about this hill beside the ninth green in the downtown park, or about Peachtree Center Plaza, or Colony Square, or that if you stand here in November when the leaves have fallen from the hickories and tulip poplars and look through the copse just behind you, you can see the white sides and small windows of my grandfather's home. Not that Mrs. Bellamy would intrude on me here if she knew. An otiose octogenarian, she leaves her apartment once monthly, and then only under my guidance, to collect the rents from her now many times subdivided family home. But if Mrs. Bellamy knew about my hill, she would surely try to eat it, would ask me questions and chew my answers into soggy morsels with her eyes until nothing here—golfers, Peachtree Center Plaza, my memory of my grandfather—could ever be entirely itself again. And these things are too important for Mrs. Bellamy.

They are, of course, not important enough for Deirdre, my wife. An unknowing disciple of Plotinus, she is largely indifferent to processes, and this is the one point on which she and Mrs. Bellamy are in accord. I have tried to explain my fears to Deirdre, have pointed out the excessive interest in heights here, the endless re-grinding of old dust, and the refusal of dead things to die, but she only smiles. Deirdre is part of the city's rising and consequently has little use for subtleties. Subtleties are for people in decline. Mrs. Bellamy and I are subtle.

"Okay, there's this old lady, and she has you go look at places."

"The Piedmont Driving Club Wednesday. Thursday, the Fox and Georgian Terrace. Friday, the Grant Park cannon battery and some colonel's home. Saturday, she wants me to visit a cemetery near Stone Mountain."

"And you just look. That's all you do. Just look."

"And read Augustine. In the park."

"But the old lady—"

"Aunty Bellamy."

"She doesn't make you read Augustine . . ."

"I read Augustine because he felt the world slipping away."

"Away from what?"

"Away."

Deirdre gazes at me with her praline-colored eyes. "I'm trying to understand, Joseph."

I smile. "Did you know that the reason Atlanta burned down so quickly the first time was Sherman's engineers didn't know about Johnston's arsenal in the railroad depot? I learned that when I visited the Swann House. Sherman was staying at the Neal home on Washington Street, and that night when the fire hit the powder magazines he thought the Confederates were shelling the city."

Deirdre continues to look at me. "And for this she pays you a hundred and ninety dollars a week?"

"And expenses."

Deirdre's eyes fall away. "I see."

Every morning Deirdre picks up her richly aged briefcase in which she carries the lavender and mauve papers that make money and pauses with her thin fingers upon the door. She is careful not to ask me how my manuscript is progressing and wishes me not a profitable or productive but only a pleasant day. This is thoughtful of her, and I am grateful. I have read somewhere that such silence is a bad state, that it can poison your life, make you morose and surly. I'm sure this is correct, though I am unable to concentrate on such thoughts for very long. Deirdre and I rarely grow cross. She smiles and touches me on the cheek before she opens the door. I watch her firm, full calves mount the steps as she walks to the car.

Tonight I stand here on this hill and allow the line from each of my four points to pass through me on the way to its opposite — Peachtree Center Plaza to grandfather's home, Colony Square to Sears, each back again. I am a vertex, an intersection of four figures in a plane and fear a sundering. Depthless, breadthless, heightless, when this concatenation breaks, will I be left to spill out into space? I watch as the lighted elevator on the Plaza's northern face climbs seventy stories to its apex and prepares to spew fluorescent semen into the night sky. There are forces here. None of us is innocent. I kick at a large upright divot as I start away.

I return to my grandfather's house where I will make supper from last week's casserole and two pears. I still call it his house though he has been dead a dozen years, the last three of which I have spent stripping woodwork and puttying cracks in a grand campaign of renovation. I sit in the garden to eat because the kitchen is littered with wallpaper, paint rollers, and tape, and spread *The Confessions* upon my knees.

Augustine shares my distrust of this city and assures me that I am a stranger here, no participant in these processes, and that there are others like me, unknown to each other, all dragging at the gravity of time. And Augustine knows something of risings and declines. Tonight I read of his walk in his garden with Alypius, of his desire for his mistress, and of his opening the testament to the fated passage: "Not in rioting and drunkeness, not in chambering and wantoness, not in strife and envying..." I hear fifteen hundred years of Western history groan at his response. For Augustine renounced love. Renounced. And who can believe a man who renounced love?

Deirdre comes home after I am in bed. I feel her crawl into the sheets beside me, but I pretend to be asleep. After a time the bare skin on our backs touches. It is tacky like the backs of damp postage stamps. We lie like that for several seconds, then I twist slowly away and fall asleep.

The great gift of classical thought as it was interpreted for the late middle ages by Berengar, Lanfranc, Anselm, Hugo of St. Victor, Abelard, Peter Lombard, Aquinas, Duns Scotus, (largely from Boethius' translation, then later from texts supplied by the Jews of Spain and Southern France, and finally after the Latin conquest of Constantinople in 1204 through direct translations from the originals)—its great gift to architecture and thus to the modern city was dialectics (especially as contained in Aristotle and in Porphyry's *Isagoge*) which in turn prepared the way for the spread of Euclidean geometry with its addiction to logical and therefore spatial precision. (Is there any relationship, one cannot help but wonder, between the intensely idealized worldview of dialectics and of math and the twelfth-century resurgence of ascetic spirituality such figures as Arnold of Brescia, and Peter of Bruys? This is only a speculation.) Whether or not, as tradition has it, the Council of Trent was truly on the verge of banning polyphonic music from the church service because of its textual unintelligibility until the performance of Palestrina's Pope Marcellus Mass—whether or not this is mere fable or hard-core historical event, Palestrina's importance (along with that of his contemporaries, Jacobus de Kerle (1531-1591) and Giovanni Animuccia (ca. 1514-1571)) cannot be exaggerated. Nor can we exaggerate the importance of this event for the eventual geometricization of the Western city. (Note for further investigation: What is the connection between the attack by the Roman church on the *unintelligibility* of the 16th-century motet and the retelling of the tower of Babel myth by Augustine in *The City of God*? According to Augustine: Babel=babble=Babylon=the city of the world. The hanging gardens as early evidence of architecture's concern with history/time (hanging=gravityless=timeless spatiality)...?)

—from an unpublished MS by
Joseph Hirschel Glisson, III

"We must become an organization, Joseph. There is something distasteful about it, but the enemy leaves us no choice." Mrs. Bellamy places her cigarette holder between her teeth and watches hungrily as I pick up the sterling lighter from the coffee table and hold the fire before her face.

"Your grandmother was a fine woman. You are a gentleman today for that fact, and I know you are grateful."

"My grandmother passed away when I was three."

"We will call ourselves the Civic Organization for the Restoration and Preservation of Society. C-O-R-P-S. We will pronounce it in the French manner. Silent 'p'."

"Like army corps."

"Precisely." She gazes over at me through the haze of smoke slithering from her nose. "I am distressed to hear about your grandmother, but your grandfather was obviously a man of uncommon breeding. No one of your mother's generation could have raised you so well."

"Perhaps if you rearranged the word order the acronym would seem less . . . ambiguous. For instance, if you simply reversed the sequence of 'Restoration and Preservation' . . ."

Mrs. Bellamy gazes over at me. "You could learn to hold yourself a bit straighter, Joseph. When gentlemen rode horses, they sat much straighter."

I adjust in my chair. "C-O-P-R-O . . . Hmmm."

"I will draw up a list and as the CORPS' amanuensis you will send the invitations."

Amanuensis?

Mrs. Bellamy smiles, pushes a slip of paper across the coffee table toward me. "Your assignment for this week."

A coincidence. Mrs. Bellamy wants me to visit the old Sears. In the morning. Before 8:30. She is insistent on this detail. If possible, I should be the first one inside. "I want to know what it is like," she says, "before the beasts and Yankee mothers trounce it up. See it fresh, Joseph."

Mrs. Bellamy does not suspect that I see the old Sears every day, that it is one of the four cusps on which my fear is hung, nor is she aware that it has an even older place in my life. I used to come here with my grandfather—for a box of screws, a ball-peen hammer, a duplicate key to the garage door lock that never seemed to work. I remember standing just outside the glass key booth at the edge of the parking lot, listening to the whine of the key-man's machine, as with one hand hanging from his drooping lapel my grandfather pointed out for me each of the four banks that formed the city's skyline.

This morning I am the third, not the first, inside. I watch a hunched woman with a shopping bag just ahead of me hobble in a determined arc toward lingerie. I roam the candy displays remembering the feathery skin of my grandfather's palm and smelling the heady stench of roasting cashews. In hardwares I stop to buy a window scraper, and a short black man with a scar across one sideburn gives me too much change. His shoulders are narrow and his jacket gathers at the back of his neck. When I show him his mistake he makes no acknowledgment, only drops the extra quarter back into the register and turns away.

On my way out I exchange smiles with a white-haired boy, hold the door for a man returning a clothes hamper. The parking lot is three-layered, concrete. It used to be asphalt, uncovered, and on a hot day like crossing a two-acre skillet. Now it is always cool.

2.

Atlantans are not trustworthy people. Watch them. They pass you on the sidewalk with hot, watery eyes. Their cheeks stream with visions. "If you are fixed on an object," they seem to say, "method pales." But I don't believe them. Even the Phoenix was stuck in cycles, returning every half-millennium to the same tree, the same altar, the same pyre. "You're caught," I want to tell them. "All of you. Caught." But they elbow past me, sweaty and heavy footed from dreaming, and disappear down crowded streets.

Before I met Mrs. Bellamy, I was a teacher of mandatory perfunctory books at a mean school for small minds. Nineteen
months ago I resigned from this position to complete a manuscript which would make me a teacher of elective, perfunctory
books at a mediocre school for average minds. My manuscript was
about architecture, class conflict, polyphony, Euclidean
geometry, mediaeval Scholasticism, the Avignon papacy, frat-
ricide, urbanization, primitive ontology, German culture before
1935, gastritis, acne, and headaches. It was a work of genius.
Approximately eighteen months and two weeks ago I stopped
work to do additional research. Eighteen months and three days
ago I began to read Augustine. Seventeen months, three weeks,
four days and some odd hours ago, I sat down at my desk to read
The City of God and in Book XV encountered these lines:
"Accordingly, it is recorded of Cain that he built a city, but Abel,
being a sojourner, built none."
Sojourner.
For the following several weeks I sat in my office each morning
and watched the titmice pick at the millet I put out on the window
ledge. In the dogwood a few feet away I saw grosbeaks, wrens, a
thrush, yellowthroats, and, once briefly, two nuthatches. I brew-
ed coffee but didn't drink it. I resharpened my pencils then placed
them unused in the earthenware cup at the corner of my desk. At
lunchtime each day Deirdre called, and I was polite. I was polite at
supper, too. And lying in bed at night staring at the small rust-
colored stains on the ceiling, I was always careful to be very still so
that Deirdre could sleep.
Mrs. Bellamy hired me because of my manuscript—and
because I was polite. Her ad read: "Opening for historian and
chauffeur. With best references." I called to interview for the
historian and was told that the ad referred to one opening, not
two. I decided that I drove well enough and needed money badly
enough to apply. I arrived on time for my interview, stood until I
was invited to sit, listened attentively, spoke in monosyllables
whenever possible, and repeatedly lit Mrs. Bellamy's cigarettes.
Mrs. Bellamy was delighted with my qualifications as well as
with the fact that I was the only applicant who appeared for his

interview.

"So you are an historian?"

"Yes."

"What sort of historian?"

"I study a number of things. Dyspepsia, for instance."

"The history of dyspepsia?"

"One of my contentions is that mild physiological distress can be related to historical processes. Dyspepsia results from an acute oversensitivity to necessity."

"It is a necessity that Atlanta remember who it is, Joseph."

"Or trauma. Often trauma occurs when new historical possibilities arise."

"*We* are Atlanta. No other point of view is possible."

"I would estimate that one-third to one-half of Italy's population was traumatized by the Avignon papacy."

"Has anyone ever told you that you resemble Henry Grady?"

"Excuse me?"

"Stand for a moment. Let me see how tall you are."

"Perhaps we should discuss my position."

"Henry Grady was a tall man. He knew a great deal about history."

"I . . . I am not quite clear yet about my responsibilities."

Mrs. Bellamy smiled, sat back and let the smoke waft up from her nostrils like a thin veil lifting before her eyes. "I, also, am an historian."

As I soon came to understand, Mrs. Bellamy's juxtaposition of chauffeur and historian was not so illogical as it had at first seemed. By "historian" Mrs. Bellamy meant a kind of tour guide to arrested moments of time, someone who, like the proprietor of a cheap roadside museum, fixes events in stone and exhibits them for the gluttonous gazes of passers-by. Though I only occasionally drove Mrs. Bellamy anywhere, I transported her constantly. I would sail out into the city with my instructions and return with these blocks of stonecast time, some actually discovered as assigned, others sculpted in accord with Mrs. Bellamy's expectations.

And Mrs. Bellamy was pleased with my work.

"You see, Joseph, we are coming to understand things, important things. And understanding is the first step toward preservation."

I, of course, understood nothing—important or unimpor-
tant—and felt poorly preserved. Afternoons I retreated to the
park where I read Augustine and where at nightfall I gazed at the
golfers, the old Sears, the Plaza's lights floating in the sky. I read
*The Catholic and the Manichaean Ways of Life, The Commen-
tary on the Lord's Sermon on the Mount with Seventeen Related
Sermons, The Confessions, On Christian Doctrine, The City of
God,* and the treatise *On the Immortality of the Soul.* I learned
about the doctrine of illumination, the principle of spirituality and
non-corporeal existence, the concepts of concupiscence and
creatio ex nihilo, and the five lusts. But each time I drove into the
city to see a crumbling monument or a condemned building or a
poorly kept grave, I recalled that cities were founded by fratricides
and that you cannot dwell in them.

I could not have explained these things to Mrs. Bellamy and
when I tried to explain them to Deirdre, she listened but afterwards only looked away and said nothing.

"Well, do you agree or disagree?" I would ask, my hands
opening and closing in my lap. "Surely, you either agree or
disagree."

"I neither agree nor disagree, Joseph."

"Surely, you have some opinion."

"No," Deirdre would say, her eyes as creamy brown as sun-
softened caramel. "It is not necessary for me to have an opinion."
And she would turn slowly and walk away.

Deirdre was, of course, correct. She had no opinion because she
had no use for one. I had opinions, attitudes, principles,
doctrines, concepts because I had little else. In the mornings I
would stare in at my desk, at the shoebox warrens of notecards,
the empty white trash can, my bent coffee spoon. The stillness of
these things disturbed me. I occasionally shuffled through some
papers but could understand little written on them. My thesis
seemed to have vanished. I would stare a moment out the win-

dow, push my desk chair aimlessly across the floor. Each time I left the room, the door closed behind me with a sucking slam.
Sojourner.

> If in Spengler's *Decline of the West* we have a portrait of the Western city painted by the agrarian mystic, in Augustine—citizen of Tagaste, Madaura, Carthage, Rome, Milan—we have the mysticism of urbanity itself. These are poles. Wirth, Park, Weber, Durkheim, all were products of urban culture. Men of thought, of intellect, they were masters of analysis but could not spiritualize urbanism any more than could Spengler.
>
> (Here we see the often deplored anachronistic and romantic character of Tillich in his 1933 socialistic writings. Tipping his hat to—while leering from behind it at—Spengler, but indirectly and more essentially in dialogue with the Nietzsche of *The Genealogy of Morals*—note triadic structure: edenic state, cultural corruption, new eden ("The Socialist Principle")—Tillich reveals that, despite his much noted cosmopolitanism and polished urbanity, he is fundamentally an agrarian viewing the forces of urbanization from the outside. It is left for the American sociologist and theologian Harvey Cox to explore the liberating power of cities, and we cannot overlook that in doing so he is driven back, understandably, to the prophets of Judah's classical period—such as Jeremiah, who shares with Charles Eduard Jeanneret ("Le Corbusier") the apocalyptic vision of life in aggregate (over against liberated space) as opposed to Frank Lloyd Wright's apotheosis of the automobile.)
>
> Their symbols were the market, the factory, the fortress, and the throne.
>
> > —from an unpublished MS by
> > Joseph Hirschel Glisson, III

Tonight Deirdre will not come home. I go to the refrigerator and find there some pineapple, not fresh, a package of cream cheese, a head of lettuce going brown. I try to eat in the garden, but October is here, and the evenings are turning cool. Inside I clear the paint pans and rollers from one end of the kitchen table and dine with *The Confessions* open beside my plate, Book XI, the meditation on time.

Augustine tells me that neither the past nor the future exists, that time is simply an extensionless point between memory and an abyss. Though utterly wrongheaded, such ideas attract me. Who hasn't at some time wanted to rise above cause and effect, to ascend to that place where possibility stretches like a plane in every direction? Still, I'm suspicious of a saint's impatience with processes. Is it so easy to complete one life, begin another? I look around me at the half-stripped wallpaper of my grandfather's dining room, the blackened furnace grates, a depression in the oak floor where a lamp table stood for thirty years. How to replenish things exhausted by time, replace old floors, walls, restore heating, plumbing? Is this rejuvenation or merely acquiescence to the past? Is it a way out or a trap?

Before going to bed I walk to the hill. Peachtree Center Plaza's glass walls glare back at me. Colony Square looms darkly beneath the moon. If I strain, I can see the flagpole on the old Sears stabbing upward into the glow from town.

I lean slowly into the darkness tonight and stretch my hands and feet to the four corners of my life. Supine like this, I cannot help but live in space. I curl my fingers about the Plaza's girth, slip one foot around the flagpole, thrust an ankle through my grandfather's kitchen window and cuddle Colony Square in my palm. My heart now is a point of convergence. The city passes down my thighs, through my chest and out my shoulders into my hands. How can we stand to be further removed from what forms us?

Some time before dawn I will wake to find myself shivering and wet with dew, my eyes hot as if from crying. I will stand and gaze out over the fairway while my mind tosses off sleep. Then I will turn slowly, slide my cold hands into my pockets, and start for home.

This happens in late October:

"Are you all right?"

I was not in bed, though I let the phone ring several times before getting up from the rocker to answer it. Deirdre's voice is husky, tense, but not unkind.

"Where are you?" I ask.

"At a friend's."

"Whose?"

She sighs impatiently. "Are you all right?"

"You haven't been home in three days."

"Four."

"Yes, I'm all right."

"How's the house?"

"I keep forgetting to be here when the plumbers come to make the estimate."

She pauses.

"I saw something tonight," I begin. "I was standing on the hill, and it was one of those evenings when the sky over Tenth Street is fuchsia and scarlet, you know."

She knows.

"And the windows in Colony Square are red. And it struck me that where the sun was going down...it was right at Marietta Street and Northside Drive."

"You can't see that far from the hill."

"I was approximating."

"Did they say they would come back?"

"They?"

"The plumbers."

"Oh, they didn't say much. It was the second time I'd missed."

I turn up the collar of my bathrobe and draw the terry cloth more tightly across my chest. Cold air is coming from somewhere. "That's where Sherman entered the city."

"What?"

"At Marietta Street and Northside Drive."

"Joseph, what are you talking about?"

The receiver feels slippery in my hand. "Sherman marched into Atlanta down Marietta Street, and the mayor met him at North-side Drive to surrender the city. And with the sky like that... it was like everything burning again."

"Sherman didn't burn the city until everyone was evacuated. That was nearly a month later." She pauses, then adds awkwardly. "How's your manuscript?"

"The same."

We are silent. When I speak, my voice is very small. "I'm dying, baby. Come home, please."

"Joseph—"

"I'm dying."

She hangs up.

Augustine's *Confessions*, Book I, Chapter 5:

"O Lord my God, tell me what you are to me. Say unto my soul; *I am thy salvation*. Speak so that I can hear. See, Lord, the ears of my heart are in front of you. Open them and say unto my soul; *I am thy salvation*. At these words I shall run and I shall take hold of you. Do not hide your face from me. Let me die, lest I should die indeed; only let me see your face."

A harvest moon tonight. From Monroe Drive the whooping of a police car breaks the stillness then fades. I stand at my back window, watch, listen. There is no wind in the garden.

"... leveled the parking lot? Why, how sensible."

"No, Mrs. Bellamy... Aunty Bellamy, they have added a level. Two levels. On the side where the key booth used to be."

Mrs. Bellamy sits very straight in the back seat of the ancient Packard and gazes at me in the rearview mirror. Her cigarette holder points upward like a lance. "Turn here."

I turn.

"Your livery needs cleaning, and your cap is dented on the left."

I reach up and pinch out my hat. When I drive Mrs. Bellamy to collect the rents, I must wear the black suit and cap which she has exhumed for me. The cloth has a strange fragrance reminiscent of formaldehyde.

"And how do they get up there?"

"Excuse me?"

"The cars. How do they get the cars up to the third level?"

"Oh...uh...there are ramps. They drive them up ramps."

"Never say 'uh.' It is vulgar." Mrs. Bellamy leans forward and rests her hand on the back of the front seat. "I have been thinking, Joseph. Perhaps I will leave Old Magnolias to the CORPS. I could call and have my will changed tomorrow afternoon. That would be helpful, don't you think? You could establish a small museum there after I am gone. And it would be our headquarters."

"Turn here?"

"Yes, yes."

The street on which "Old Magnolias" stands is an embarrassed street, embarrassed because it knows that it is untrue and because it knows that I can see this. Its boxwoods and chrysanthemums are untrue, as are its English-ivy-covered bricks and its incongruous clusters of Victorian traceries, Palladian enclaves, Romanesque crenelations, Ionic columns, classical porticoes, Tudor half-timbered gables, rococo balconies. This is Pericles' Athens, the street announces. This is seventeenth-century Versailles or the Italy of the Medicis or at the very least, a fine Southern city of a century and a quarter ago. The gargoyles climb down from the wrought-iron gates and slink away as I turn up the drive.

"The grounds have been well maintained, Joseph. It would be a simple matter for you to put down a few walks, restore the period furnishings, rope off the displays. As the CORPS' executive director you could have your office in the parlor. And in back we could erect a display of the barbarians burning down the Georgia Railroad Depot just as—"

I stop the car. "Are you sure you don't want me to collect for you today? You could wait in the car."

Mrs. Bellamy lavishes upon me a wilting stare. "*I am the owner.*"

The interior of "Old Magnolias" is less untrue than the facade and grounds. The carpet is tired, as are the balustrade and stairs, and the hollow-core doors advertise their poverty. I knock at the first apartment.

"Of course, you might prefer to have your office on one of the upper floors."

"The parlor would be fine."

"From the upper floor you could see the grounds more easily."

"Renovating the upper floors would be more expensive."

"Petty concerns."

"I'm sure the organization's budget will be limited. There's no answer."

"Leave them a card."

I take from my coat pocket one of Mrs. Bellamy's cards which informs the tenant that he or she has missed the rent appointment, that Mrs. Bellamy is displeased and that the rent check must be personally delivered within the week, and slip it under the door.

"The problem today, Joseph, is that there is no feeling for quality."

"Yes."

"No people of quality; no families of quality; no homes of quality."

"Mmmhmm."

"Old Magnolias has quality. That's why we must preserve it."

A guitar is screeching in the next apartment. I knock on the door. An anemic, shirtless boy appears before me.

"Mrs. Bellamy is here to collect the rent."

"Harry ain't home."

From behind me: "No more of that disgraceful racket; tell Mr. Brooks he has missed his appointment and is late with his rent; get dressed."

We start up the stairs.

"You see, a museum sets an example. It shows the unlearned that what we are cannot be avoided."

"Some of the unlearned seem to have avoided what 'we' are quite successfully."

"I'm speaking now only of people of breeding, people of good families."

"The unlearned of good families?"

"A museum preserves what is fine, what is timeless. It is a fortress against the onslaught of a tawdry age."

"Restoring these halls would be difficult. I don't think this molding is made anymore."

"Sacrifices will be required. Our soldiers have always been willing to make sacrifices for quality."

The next door is opened by a young Negro woman in linen trousers with skin the color of cafe au lait.

"Mrs. Bellamy is here to collect the rent," I say.

Mrs. Bellamy makes an impatient rumble in her throat. "Inform Mr. Fischer that Mrs. Bellamy is here."

The young woman eyes Mrs. Bellamy a second longer than is polite, then disappears.

"You see, Joseph, everyone today is confused. No one knows what he is. The South is in the power of degenerates. Even the nigras are being turned into scoundrels. You cannot hire a nigra with breeding any more."

I can see into the foyer. There is a large Vasarely poster on a gallery-white wall. The floors are polished and bare.

"When you establish the museum, Joseph, you must make all the nigras wear uniforms. I have noticed that nothing makes a servant so conscious of the dignity of his position as much as a smart, new uniform."

The young woman reappears with a check extended in her hand. "Two eighty-five?" she asks with manifold insouciance. "Alan wasn't sure."

I nod, take the check.

"Tell Mr. Fischer that Mrs. Bel—"

The door closes quietly.

Mrs. Bellamy and I stand side by side in the empty hall. "A uniform would make a great difference," she adds.

"Yes." We start back down the steps.

Polyphony with its great complexity and expansion
of mathematical possibilities (especially with the practical disappearance of the Celtic pentatonic) demanded
that its practitioners maintain a mathematician's
rigorous control over harmonic intervals. (Note here
the use of spatial and mathematical analogies in music
theory: interval, distance, high, low, even the num-
bering of the points on the scale and the fractioning of
metrics—quarter note, eighth note.) Though still
without much of the elaborate apparatus of tonality,
dominance/subdominance, chromatic and enhar-
monic counterpoint, and the mathematicization of
intervals, the musicians of the late middle ages and
early   Renaissance—from   Hucbalds'   *Musica
Enchiriadis* in the tenth century to the theoretical writing of Johannes Tinctoris in the 15th and 16th
centuries—already had begun to lay down basic rules
of scale, proportion, and the rigors of acceptable and
unacceptable melisma and improvisation (*basso continuo*). Just as this was a musical mathematics fueled
both by the Scholasticism of the mediaeval church and
by the rediscovery of classical learning, so it was one
which the greatest of architects, Andrea di Pietro della
Gondola Palladio, could look to as a symbol of all that
was appropriate in formal elegance. (One cannot avoid
the   speculation   that   Palladio's   fixation   on
"harmony"—here space reverses the former process
and borrows from music—with its attendant concepts
of symmetry and proportion—remember that Palladio derived his theory of proportions not from Euclid
directly but from polyphony—one cannot avoid the
speculation that Palladio's aesthetic formulas are in an
indirect line of descent from Plato's formal concepts as
interpreted by Plotinus' *Enneads* ("Beauty") and
reformulated by Augustine and afterwards filtered
through the Aristotelianism of Hugo of St. Victor and
Aquinas. And from here we are led unavoidably to
wonder to what extent this locking into a mathematical system, with its consequent proscription of imaginable possibilities, is related to that famous blockage of

Luther's colon, that massive constipation with a rigorous and dysfunctional historical necessity which evacuated itself explosively on the door of the castle church in Wittenberg on October 31, 1517. Which only raises once again the psychophysiological problem of revolution itself and brings to mind the *Cordeliers* in 1789 and particularly the dermatitis of Jean Paul Marat. Another interesting case.)

—from an unpublished MS by
Joseph Hirschel Glisson, III

"Nice day for the park."

I look up from the page. I didn't hear Deirdre approach. "Wind is chilly."

I slide over in the swing. The chains sing under the added weight.

"Augustine?" she asks nodding at my book.

"*On the Immortality of the Soul.*"

She nods.

"Haven't seen you in awhile," I say.

"I come by during the day. You're out."

"Work all right?"

"Nothing changes. You're still working for the old lady?"

"Mrs. Bellamy."

"*Aunty* Bellamy," she corrects me with a smile.

"Mmhmmm, but I don't know for how long."

She leans back, pushes off the ground with her feet. We begin to swing slowly. "Did I ever tell you that I read *The Confessions* in college?"

"No. When?"

"I don't think we were dating then. It was an abnormal psychology course." She turns to face me. "You know, he was in love with his mother."

" 'It is impossible that the son of these tears should perish.' "

"What?"

"That's what a bishop told her once. To get rid of her. She

worried so much over his soul—Augustine's—that she nearly drove the bishop crazy."

I shift in my seat. "Augustine and Monica. That was her name. Monica."

"My psychology professor tried to argue that Augustine was abnormal but not unhealthy."

"Neoplatonism. The ladder of love. Love of a particular woman, love of the ideal woman, love of beauty itself, love of harmony the essence of beauty, love of the Good, love of God, love of absolute unity, and so forth. Plotinus takes the ladder image from 'The Symposium.'"

"I don't remember."

"The mother thing is curious."

"Hmmm?"

"Well, you can't miss that a lot of erotic energy is being displaced in Augustine. But love—think about it—love exists outside of time. Lovers are oblivious to time. Now, if Augustine refused to be a lover—at least in the conventional sense—why did he become so absorbed with cities? Why didn't the displaced love—"

"Joseph, why do you keep reading this?"

"I thought you were interested."

"But why do you read it?"

I shrug. "Why do anything? Why did you come to the park today?"

"Because I wanted to see you."

I gaze out over the duck pond toward the golf course. The wind brushes my cheeks as we swing slowly forward and back. "I don't know why I read it."

"I guess you aren't working on the house anymore."

"No."

"Do you eat well?"

"Well enough."

We fall silent. After a time I stand. "I'm going to the hill. The sun will set before long."

She nods. "I'm going to stay here awhile."

"Thanks for finding me."

We gaze at each other, then Deirdre lowers her eyes. "It wasn't like running out."

"No." My throat feels very dry. "It wasn't like that at all." I stand in silence a moment more, then start away.

Mrs. Bellamy wants me to go to the Loew's Grand Theatre, to see a movie there, any movie, to stand in the lobby, to push down the nap on the scarlet carpeting with the toe of my shoe, to smudge my thumbprint across the polished brass doorknobs, to smell popcorn and ask for seating assistance from any of the nattily dressed young men who glide up and down the aisles. I, of course, agree.

I catch a Thirty-one bus up Peachtree, get off at Margaret Mitchell Square, turn my back on the Atlanta Public Library and center my feet in the same square of concrete onto which Vivien Leigh stepped when she climbed from her limousine, tossed her roan-red hair over one shoulder and with a smirk stalked past the police cordon into the foyer. I stand a moment staring at the plywood fence which borders the sidewalk, at a tangle of black teenagers laughing in the shade of a magazine stand, at the expanse of gray sky. The walk is rain spotted and a cold breeze blows down Forsyth Street. Then I start up the block.

I recall how many times I walked these blocks with my grand-father, how often we climbed from the bus together and I clung to his hand as he led me to the Cable Piano Company for my weekly music lesson. It was an old block then, and I remember the demo-lition of the first buildings and the emergence in their place of new structures, white box-shaped things. Each week my grandfather and I stood at the windows just outside my teacher's cork-board office and watched the concrete forms and steel I-beams pile up story on story, at first gazing down at them, then looking directly over at the workmen across the expanse of Peachtree, then gradu-ally craning to look up, up, until finally the workmen were beyond seeing, so that it became a simple act of faith to believe they were still up there, completing the work we had watched begun.

The Cable Piano Company has long since been replaced by two sand-colored office towers. The shop where I used to browse over art supplies is now a flat promenade leading to a glass-domed shopping mall two stories below the street. The soda fountain where I waited for the bus is a forty-foot bronze sculpture. Just up the block Peachtree Center Plaza stretches out of sight.

I do not know if I will tell Mrs. Bellamy that the Loew's Grand Theatre has burned down. I am not certain whether I will explain that the foyer is a red mud ditch filled with charred brick and lumber, that the scene of the premiere of the world's most famous movie has been torched by vandals, that within a year it will be a disembarking point for the Metro Atlanta Rapid Transit Authority subway system—no, I do not know if I will tell her these things.

Standing in the lobby of the Plaza I gaze up at the columnea and German ivy trailing from the interior balconies, listen to the water trickling into the pond which forms the lobby floor, watch the transparent elevators float noiselessly upward. On my way out I pass, coming in, a young woman whom I remember fondly from another time. She holds herself erect, carries under one arm a cordovan purse. Her hair is pulled behind her head into a fine black bun. I watch her approaching, smile. My hand lifts in greeting. She stares long and hard but passes making no sign. I continue on out of the foyer, then hesitate, glance down at myself. The knees of my trousers are soiled; my shirt is wrinkled (Did I sleep in it last night?). I do not remember when last I shaved.

If we view mediaeval mysticism as the conjunction of a relatively crude, highly practical, non-spiritualistic religion (Hebraism, it should be recalled, had no doctrine of the soul until shortly before the time of the Maccabees—the concept of "shades" being probably a digression rather than an early point in a continuous development) with the aethereal consciousness of the Alexandrians (Egypt here representing the Westernmost movement of Eastern spiritual-

ity), if we view early Christian mysticism in this manner, then Augustine's Trinitarian formula and his role
in the Pellagian controversy become, if no more
rational, at least more humanly understandable, and
certainly their fundamental relation to his Neo-
platonic urbanism becomes clearer. Whereas Tertul-
lian, Origen, and Athanasius had taught the subordi-
nation of the Son and the Spirit to the Father, Augustine so insisted on the unity of the Godhead as to teach
a full equality of persons. Here we see the mystical
consciousness with its delight in antinomy, paradox,
dialectical opposition, apparent contradiction, over
against the earliest expressions of the urban consciousness with its faith in bureaucratic organization, hierar-
chy, rationally determined lines of authority and
responsibility. Unitarianism versus Trinitarianism is
nothing other than the collision of two continuously
opposed perspectives on the Fall.

—from an unpublished MS by
Joseph Hirschel Glisson, III

3.

You leave Atlanta in November. It is not a safe place to be when
winter comes. Everyone knows that dreamers cannot endure
cold, and no one here can be trusted with a fire. Still, there is little
good to say for those who remain. They are not courageous so
much as bovine—the witless courage of cows. Was there anything admirable in the Phoenix's act? I can't see it. A great deal of
show just to remain as he was. But he cheated time that way, and
something must be said for that.

I come to my hill once more. The golfers now are only two old
men, stiff-kneed in British racing caps, three-putting the ninth
green. They watch one another as each in turn bends and pushes
his ball a little closer to the hole. Just past the clubhouse my car

waits at the curb. It is stuffed with essential things—papers, shoeboxes of notecards, Augustine, my desk, my chair. It seems poised for flight, but I find myself dawdling. Leaving cities is a little like dying, I think. The whiteness of empty rooms startles you. Theirs is the beauty of bodies when the soul has flown. I see a football team scrimmaging in the high school stadium. Cars sail up and down Tenth Street. You cannot help but wonder; am I leaving something behind?

"I was a young lady, Joseph, when 'Gone with the Wind' premiered."

Yes, of course, I am leaving something behind.

"I stood right where you stood, with my father who was an alderman at the time and beside Judge Cox and when Clark Gable strode by, Joseph, he was such a gentleman, he tipped his hat to me. Nothing brash or untoward, you understand. He recognized me for a lady, and was gallant."

"Nothing has changed."

Mrs. Bellamy bites down on her cigarette holder, sucks smoke through her teeth. "Of course, I certainly did not act like those foolish girls whose families had pushed them up to the front of the lines. There was a disgraceful amount of blushing and simpering around me."

"The Loew's Grand Theatre is perfectly preserved."

"For my part, I gave him a smile, only a courteous smile. Then I turned my head."

"I am going away, Mrs. Bellamy."

Mrs. Bellamy leans forward. "I heard rumors that there had been a fire..."

I shake my head. "Nothing is changed. Even the brass doorknobs are still shining."

She smiles, reclines into a cloud of smoke. "He was a tall man. His shoulders were very straight."

"Is there anything else—"

"Perhaps as resident historian of the CORPS you could request that the Loews make a contribution to our museum. Something from the premiere, a memento. After all, preservation is in everyone's best interest."

"Yes."

"And you say the brass still shines?"

"Brightly."

"We are Atlanta, Joseph."

"I am leaving."

Mrs. Bellamy pushes the sheet of paper across the coffee table toward me. "Don't forget your assignment."

I gaze at the paper silently.

"It is a shame I never met your grandfather. His name was?"

"Joseph; like mine."

She nods hungrily. "A gentleman's name."

"He sold insurance. He did not do well."

"A tall man. Did he ride horses?"

"His hair was thin and white, and he spoke in a small voice."

"And he taught you gentleness with ladies."

I rest my hand on the knob of the door. "Yes, Mrs. —Aunty Bellamy. Gentleness with ladies."

There is a noise behind me, but I do not stop. I hurry out to my car and do not allow myself to think again until I am here gazing down at these two golfers straggling back to the clubhouse just below my shoes.

What did Augustine say? "But how one must condemn the river of human custom! Who can stand firm against it? When will it ever dry up? How long will it continue to sweep the Sons of Eve into that huge and fearful ocean...?" Time, history, that fear of the ineluctible slide. But where are there voices now, gardens, holy words, anything which speaks to us from beyond it?

It is mid-afternoon, and the facets of Peachtree Center Plaza reflect the sunlight into the streets. This is an insane place, I tell myself. A city of lovers. I resist an urge to dust my shoes and curse. Through the copse I can now see clearly the side of my grandfather's house. It is badly weathered. Before it can be sold there will need to be some repairs. The wind is low, and on the flagpole of the old Sears the flag hardly moves. I will stop by Colony Square on my way out of town.

Deirdre has her office there. She sees me from her third-floor window, comes down to meet me at the street, stands smiling.

Her cheeks are sunburned, and I think how fine she looks and how well she will grow old. We talk of inconsequential things. She inspects the car. For a few seconds we fall silent and look down the street.

Deirdre believes in the present, mine as well as hers, sees it stretching out endlessly around her. She does not believe possibility ever comes to a close. She tells me I will finish my book. She tells me to say only necessary things.

I tell her my manuscript is full of mistakes.

Deirdre smiles and strokes my arm. "There are no mistakes, Joseph."

At the corner, before turning, I stop and look back. She is still there. We gaze at each other for a long time. We do not wave.

(1)4.

Riding out of Atlanta I fall in with a family of women, all ages, heading east. I'm lucky enough to have my horse still, and I consider offering to let one of them ride but have no idea which one. The dust is already hot and thick this morning. I cover my mouth with my hand, turn away, cough and spit. They don't seem to notice. Behind us from the direction of the depot come occasional explosions. When the fire reaches Joe Johnston's arsenal, everything from Whitehall to Spring Street is going to blow. I look over my shoulder. Five Points is a fist of smoke.

"You!"

I feel a tugging at my trouser leg, turn swiftly expecting to see a Yankee sentry but look down instead into the splotched and dusty face of a young woman.

"You know what day this is?"

I nod. "Yes, ma'm. November fourteen." I hesitate, then add, "My birthday."

"Then you don't forget. Yankee dirt took our horses, killed our chickens, burnt us out. On your birthday."

Her hair has come loose on one side and is hanging over her

shoulder. I notice now for the first time she holds a child wrapped in a scarf in the crook of one arm. I rein my horse.

"If you'd like to ride, ma'm..."

She doesn't hear me, just hangs onto my trouser leg, stares into my face.

"Decatur's not far up ahead," I add. "Folks'll put you up there."

"On your birthday."

I lean closer. "They burned my place too, ma'm. But it'll be all right."

FICTION COLLECTIVE
Books in Print

Flatiron Book Distributors Inc., 175 Fifth Avenue (Suite 814), NYC 10010